TERROR IN THE SHADOWS

PIERCE MOSTYN PARANORMAL INVESTIGATIONS
BOOK 3

C W HAWES

CWH BOOKS

✤ Formatted with Vellum

For my daughter

ENTER THE IMAGINATIVE WORLD OF CW HAWES

Enter my world. A world of terror on a cosmic scale. Just click, tap, or scan the QR code below.

Fear is the most primal of human emotions. And fear of the unknown is the most terrifying of all fears.

If you are new to the Pierce Mostyn Paranormal

Investigations series, then *Terror in the Shadows* is an excellent entry point into the series and into my world.

In addition to my Pierce Mostyn Paranormal Investigations books, I've written short stories set in the world of the macabre and arcane. Many of which are only available to folks on my mailing list.

So just click, tap, or scan the QR code to enter my world of terror and the macabre. You will get a free copy of *The Feeder* and you'll get my monthly email of news and curated contact. Terror awaits!

1

_____

THE COUNTRYSIDE WAS BEAUTIFUL. Lushly green. Hilly. The black, unmarked SUV made its way westward along I-68, crossing into West Virginia just after nine on a sunny morning in July.

Special Agent in Charge Pierce Mostyn was sitting in the second row of seats with Doctor Jeffrey Mansfield, a specialist in genetically caused physical deformities.

In the front, driving, was Special Agent DC Jones. Sitting next to Jones was photographer Willie Lee Baker, who with camera at the ready, was snapping pictures of the countryside.

In the third row of seats Doctor Dotty Kemper, a forensic anthropologist, perhaps _the_ forensic anthropologist in the world, and Doctor Arliss Cashel, an ethnologist, were debating just how modern Neanderthal humans actually were.

Mostyn turned his attention from the scenery back to the report he'd been given by Doctor Rafe Bardon, director of the most secret of the government's secret agencies: the Office of Unidentified Phenomena, or OUP for short.

The report contained an account from the 1920s concerning the Martense family and their mansion in the Catskills of New York State. There was another account of an incident similar to the Martense situation from the 1940s that had occurred in the Appalachian region of northern Georgia, and another from the 1970s in the same area. And lastly there were the accounts from West Virginia, deep in the heart of Appalachia. The area to which Mostyn and his team were headed.

The 1920s account came from an amateur aficionado of the arcane and the macabre who had stumbled on the horror that had become the Martense family and when his findings fell into the hands of certain government agents, it was then that the Federal government took an interest in several mysterious disappearances and murders in the Catskill region.

As the government had responded to the sinister events at Innsmouth, so too they responded to the situation on Tempest Mountain. To this day, in secret facilities around the country, scientists study the beings that are genetically related to old Gerrit Martense.

Mostyn looked out the window. The country through which they were driving could be described as nothing less than idyllic. Yet in all of the United States there are areas no more remote or unknown than parts of Appalachia.

In spite of the relatively low height of the mountains, the region possesses some of the most rugged and nearly inaccessible terrain on earth.

From the beauty of the passing scenery, Mostyn once again turned his gaze back to the report. From the Catskills to Georgia, the same occurrences of cannibalism and human carnage had been reported.

As abruptly as the Georgia horror had begun, in the 1940s, it had ended, news reaching the Federal government too late for war-stretched agencies to do anything about it. Then thirty years later, in the same area, bizarre tales of cannibalism and of the inhabitants of several small communities being torn apart on dark, storm tormented nights. Only blood and body parts being found in the morning.

And once again, as abruptly as the atrocities began, they ceased, news reaching Federal ears too late for any kind of government intervention. These accounts, along with many others, were passed on to the OUP when it was created. This time, however, word reached Doctor Bardon's ears almost before it had reached the media. And when it did, Doctor Bardon jumped on it.

Mostyn read about the three reported incidents that had occurred so far this year in West Virginia, the four that had occurred last year, and the one the year before that. Brutal murders. Evidence of cannibalism. Vague reports of hairy, beast-like creatures that walked upright with an oddly human gait.

Around him were the sounds of Baker's camera, Kemper's and Cashel's discussion, and Jones softly singing some '80s song. Somewhere out there, in the lush greenery of the hills they were passing through, was a hidden horror, a lurking fear that was terrorizing the people in the vicinity of the hamlet called Heirloom, West Virginia.

Four days ago, in the middle of a wild nighttime thunderstorm, was the most recent occurrence. In the little unincorporated village of Shiloh, located several miles to the southeast of Heirloom, a witness reported seeing at least half a dozen shapes, "things" the witness had called them, come out of the dense forest. That's all the person saw because he'd found his missing dog and was on his way home.

The next day, however, the entire community quickly became aware of the disaster that had struck in the night. The Ardilla and Bosk families had been murdered in their sleep and eaten. Raw. The perpetrators showed no concern about hiding the dead or of concealing evidence. The county sheriff got numerous fingerprints, handprints, and casts of bare feet. Samples of hair were also collected. The forensic analysis concluded the hair was human, as well as the teeth marks on the bones.

And that's when Doctor Bardon stepped in and claimed jurisdiction. Mostyn looked at Bardon's small neat script and read his conclusion:

The incidents in the Catskills and those that occurred in Georgia in the 1940s and 1970s are too similar to these current incidents to ignore. Your mission is to determine the source, assess the danger level, and take appropriate action to eliminate the threat, if a threat exists, to the United States of America.

Mostyn's gaze returned to the scenery outside his window. Somewhere out there was a horror that had been quietly at work for nearly a hundred years. Perhaps more. A horror hidden in the shadows of this beautiful paradise.

2

Because Heirloom was a dying unincorporated village on the banks of the Ohio River, its glory days long gone, gone with the end of West Virginia coal mining, there were no hotels or restaurants in town. Just a small coffee shop and convenience store. Therefore, Herndon, the accounting wonk who'd made the arrangements, had gotten reservations for Mostyn's team in New Martinsville, West Virginia, some fifteen and a half miles to the northeast of Heirloom.

When Jones drove into New Martinsville, Mostyn could see easily enough that this town wasn't dying. It boasted half a dozen hotels and motels and a Walmart. Herndon had booked them into the Holiday Inn. He'd also given them their IDs and credit cards for this mission. They were agents from the Department of Health and Human Services's Office of Inspector General. Their cover story was they were investigating the possibilities of disease from the dangerous wild animal attacks.

Since the time was shortly after one in the afternoon, Mostyn thought it would be best to get lunch before driving over to the county sheriff's office in Middlebourne. Upon the desk clerk's recommendation, he had Jones drive the team over to the local Bob Evans restaurant, famous for their homestyle farmhouse menu.

"Oh, for God's sake, Mostyn," Kemper blurted out when she heard where they were going for lunch. "You can't be serious?"

Mansfield asked what was wrong with the food at Bob Evans. Jones said he hoped they had country fried steak. Baker thought their fried chicken was good.

Kemper shook her head, and muttered, "Men!"

Cashel laughed, and said, "Oh, Dot. You know the quickest way to a man's heart is through his stomach. And they like good ol' comfort food best."

Seeing she was outnumbered, Kemper stopped talking and resorted to pouting.

At the restaurant, the team gathered around a table and a waitress came over to take their orders.

Jones got his country fried steak, mashed potatoes and country gravy. And Baker, his fried chicken. Mansfield ordered a soup and sandwich combo and Cashel, a slow-roasted ham and cheese sandwich.

"Well, Kemper, what tickles your taste buds?" Mostyn asked.

"The Green Goddess salad," she replied.

He nodded at her response and said he'd have the same plus a bowl of chili.

When the waitress left, Mansfield asked Mostyn how they were going to proceed.

"We'll check in with the sheriff and let him know we're conducting an investigation. Perhaps get some information while we're at it, provided he's not too territorial. Then we'll interview the locals."

"I thought we already had information on each of the incidences?" Kemper said.

"We do," Mostyn replied. "Can't beat talking to the local authorities, though. Things have a way of not appearing in reports. Plus your man on the street will have heard all manner of gossip and urban legends. Some of which may be useful."

"If this is anything like what happened in those previous accounts, this is going to be a rare opportunity to study human regression." Mansfield's voice and demeanor radiated excitement.

Kemper uttered a wry chuckle. "The infamous abhuman of gothic fiction."

"You mock, Doctor Kemper, but there is no reason why genetics must always advance and we do know that inbreeding, for instance, generates genetic abnormalities at a higher rate than outbreeding."

"All very true, Doctor Mansfield," Kemper replied. "However, we've yet to actually find a true example of a so-called abhuman."

Mansfield smiled. "Righto. This seems our best chance. Although you are forgetting the Martense family investigation."

Kemper's face took on a look of disgust. "So secret no one can get near to the scientists working on the project."

"Indeed," Mansfield concurred. "So perhaps we now have the opportunity for our own pet project."

"*Your* pet project. *If* these abhumans truly exist."

Mansfield merely shrugged in response to Kemper's comment.

The conversation paused while the waitress arrived with their food. When she left there was a lull while everyone began eating, which didn't end until everyone was more or less finished.

"Sorry we don't have time for dessert," Mostyn said, "but we need to get to the sheriff's office."

He paid the bill and they filed out of the restaurant and got back into the SUV. Jones set the GPS and followed the directions the British English voice gave him to the county seat of Tyler County.

West Virginia 180 wound its way through heavily wooded and hilly country. There were plenty of signs of people. Mobile homes, churches, Ma and Pa businesses, houses, and cars. Although there were stretches of highway that seemed to have been carved through great swaths of dark primeval forest.

"Sure wouldn't want to get a flat tire here," Kemper said.

Jones quipped, "I wouldn't want one anywhere."

"You would miss the point," Kemper shot back.

Looking in the rearview mirror, Jones asked, "Don't you ever get tired of being nasty?"

Before Kemper replied, Mostyn, his voice tinged with a

stern edge, said, "Enough. Change the subject." And that put the damper on any talk until they arrived in Middlebourne.

Once in the county seat, Cashel said, "Looks like any other small town."

"That it does," Baker agreed.

Houses, shops, and stores lined Main Street. And just passed the Dollar General was the county courthouse building.

"Look at that!" Mansfield exclaimed. "A clocktower!"

Jones parked, everyone got out of the SUV, and walked into the big old building. The directory informed them the sheriff's office was in the back of the building and that's where Mostyn and his team went.

Sheriff L. W. Elswick was in and agreed to see them.

"What can I do for you, Mr. Mostyn?"

"We're from the Office of the Inspector General of the Department of Health and Human Services." Mostyn showed the sheriff his credentials. "This is my team." And he introduced everyone.

"I'm not aware of any health problem," Elswick said. "Is there a welfare problem?"

Mostyn smiled. "We're here to investigate the possibility of contagious disease from the vicious animal attacks that have occurred."

"I see." The sheriff was hesitant.

"Is there a problem, Sheriff?" Mostyn asked.

"No, not really. Although we might not be dealing with animals."

"No?"

"No. There are indications, from marks on the bones of some of the victims, that the attackers were human."

"I see. Are you saying there are indications of cannibalism?"

"That's what I'm saying, Special Agent Mostyn."

Mansfield spoke. "There are a few rare diseases that can afflict humans and cause them to act in this manner. And those diseases can be contagious. So even if the killer is human, these cases would still fall within our purview."

"Okay. Are you joining our investigation?"

Mostyn knew that tone of voice. It was that of the local authority resenting federal intrusion onto their turf.

"No, we aren't," he replied. "We would like to talk to those involved and see what you've come up with thus far. But we aren't horning in. We'll be conducting our own investigation independent of yours. And I'll be more than happy to share with you anything we think might be of help to you."

The sheriff breathed a visible sigh of relief. "I'd like that. And we'll share what we have, if it will help you."

"Very good. Do you have time to talk now?"

The next forty-five minutes were spent with the sheriff telling Mostyn and his people about the incidents and answering their questions.

The information was mostly a repeat of what they'd already read in the files from Bardon. There had been fourteen brutal attacks going back three years with three of those attacks occurring this year. The number of victims had increased with each year and each attack, evidence that the perpetrators were getting bolder.

Both local and FBI forensics had verified human teeth markings on numerous bones, which indicated both cannibalism and the existence of at least six different perpetrators and that they were probably working together.

The sheriff ran his fingers through his hair. "Quite honestly, the bodies are piling up. Four days ago, ten people died over there in Shiloh. Two families completely wiped out. And it was grizzly. Bodies just ripped apart. Whatever these things are, whatever is causing them to do what they're doing, must be stopped. I have a near panic situation on my hands here."

"We'll do what we can, Sheriff," Mostyn assured him.

Kemper spoke, "I'd like to examine the bodies, Sheriff, if I may."

"You're the forensic anthropologist, right? Doctor Kemper?"

"I am."

"Doctor Arrington is pretty good. I can give you his report."

Kemper stepped up to the sheriff's desk and put her hands on it so her face was close to Elswick's. "I'm the best goddamn forensic anthropologist on this planet and I'd like to take a look at the bodies myself."

Mostyn could tell the sheriff was getting ready for a fight. He stepped forward and gently touched Kemper's shoulder. She straightened and took a step back.

"It would help us if Doctor Kemper could draw her own conclusions," Mostyn explained, his voice placating. "Then she could compare her conclusions with your Doctor Arrington's."

"I'll see what I can arrange." Elswick turned from Kemper and looked at Mostyn. "Call me in the morning and I'll let you know."

"Thanks, Sheriff," Mostyn said. "We'll get out of your hair now."

Mostyn and Elswick shook hands. Mostyn turned to his team and said, "Let's hit the road."

Once outside the Sheriff's office, Mostyn told the others to go on out to the SUV and that he and Dotty would be along shortly.

She stopped, and, with fists on her hips, faced Mostyn. "Are you going to chew me out for what I said back there?"

"Huh? Uh, no. No."

"Well, what then?"

Mostyn motioned they should start walking and he and Kemper slowly made their way to the front door.

"Us. Dotty. I'm sorry. I did what I had to do to get everyone back."

She stopped and faced him. Her eyes blazed for a moment, then she relaxed. "I know, Pierce. I... I..."

"You need more time."

She nodded.

"Okay. I can give you more time. If there had been any other way, I swear..."

"You did what you needed to do. You, yourself, have always said our job, the OUP and what we do, is bigger and more important than us. We are expendable. That's true, but a woman doesn't want to think that includes love. It's the stuff of romance novels. Our book boyfriends."

Mostyn started to speak, but she raised her hand to

silence him. "I had feelings for you for a long time, Pierce. Because of our work, I hid them. But after Agate Bay and the shoggoth, I, well, I decided life's too short."

"Yes," Mostyn agreed.

"Intellectually, I know you had sex with the K'nyanian to secure her help. You used her to get us free. And it worked. But my heart knows she loves you. Even after she knew you were using her, she came back just so she could come to our world. And I think she did so just to be with you. Why? Because she loves you. And, well, I think you care about her. I'm not a nice person, Pierce."

"Dotty, that's—"

She laid a finger on his lips. "No, it's true. I'm mean, cranky, and irascible."

"Dotty, I love you. I want—"

She shook her head. "Not now. Maybe tomorrow. Maybe never. I don't know." She looked into his eyes and then leaned in and kissed his cheek. "I still care. So maybe. Come on, the others are going to think we're lost."

They walked on out to the SUV and got in.

"Where to, Boss?" Jones asked.

Mostyn looked at his watch. "I think we're done for today. Tomorrow, we'll start talking to people."

"Sounds good to me," Jones said, and turned the big SUV around and drove back to New Martinsville.

Once out of town, Mostyn looked out on the lush green vegetation. Dense, almost impenetrable. He thought of the subterranean world of K'n-yan, starless, sunless, forever bathed in blue light. Two worlds so very, very different from each other.

He'd last seen H'tha-dub a month ago. Her name now Helene Dubreuil. A consultant and agent in the Office of Unidentified Phenomena. And, yes, she was still in love with him and continued to call him her husband.

Out there, hidden in the beautiful green world, bathed by sun and moon and stars, was another terror, another horror. His life was filled with horror. But for a short time there'd been love and he liked it. He liked it a lot.

3

IN THE MORNING, Mostyn called Sheriff Elswick and was told Doctor Kemper could examine the bodies. Mostyn thanked him and informed Kemper. He chuckled when he saw her eyes light up.

The drive from New Martinsville, after breakfast at Bob Evans, didn't take long. The air was already sticky at 9 o'clock and with the sun brightly shining, the day was gearing up to be a real cooker.

Dotting the route, starting about a mile outside Heirloom, were houses, mobile homes, churches, a few businesses, and abandoned buildings. Everything had the subtle feel of neglect and decay about it.

"This has to be the most goddamned depressing sight," Kemper said.

"Welcome to Appalachia," Cashel replied.

"Been here before?" Jones asked.

"If you'd read through your assignment, Jones, you'd know the answer," Mostyn chided.

"C'mon, Mostyn. Do you have to be such a spoil sport?" Baker scolded. "He's trying to find a pickup line."

Mansfield chuckled. "I'll help you out, Jones."

"Thanks, Doc."

Mansfield continued, "What were you researching here, Arliss? I don't recall the dossier telling us that."

"I was researching ethnic distribution and its effect on local dialects," Cashel replied. "I was in West Virginia, but on the other side of the state."

"What did you conclude?" Jones asked.

"There was an impact. Local dialects reflect the ethnic origin of the immigrant population to the area."

"Pretty heady stuff," Jones said.

"I am a pretty heady girl," Cashel replied.

"I agree on the pretty part," Jones said, his eyes on the rearview mirror.

"Keep your eyes on the road, Jones," Mostyn said.

"Man, Mostyn, you're worse than my father," Jones complained.

Laughter rippled through the vehicle.

West Virginia 2 formed Heirloom's Main Street. Not quite in the middle of the hamlet, the Heirloom Road led off into the hill country. The village itself was sandwiched between the Ohio River and the forested hills that piled up to the southeast.

Once inside the unincorporated town's border, Jones slowed down to fifteen miles per hour.

"Where do we start, Boss?" Jones asked.

"Not sure. Drive through town, turn around, and drive back."

Once Heirloom was behind them, Jones sped up, made a U turn a couple miles down the road, and drove back.

"Stop at the Methodist Church there," Mostyn said. "I think we'll start with…" He took a slip of paper out of his pocket. "We'll start with Obed Gillies. He saw something six days ago. Two days before the last attack. He's become something of a local celebrity since the attack in Shiloh."

Jones pulled into the small parking lot. One car, a Toyota, was there, parked up by the church, and Jones pulled in next to it.

Mostyn opened his door. "Cashel, you're with me." And he exited the vehicle.

Arliss Cashel got out, ran her hands down her blouse and the top of her slacks, and followed Mostyn into the church.

The building appeared empty and Mostyn called out, "Hello! Anybody here?"

After a few moments an older woman appeared. "May I help you?"

"Yes," Mostyn replied. "I'm Pierce Mostyn and this is Arliss Cashel. We are looking for a man by the name of Obed Gillies. Do you know where he lives?"

"I'm Reverend May Altmeyer. He's not a member here, but Heirloom isn't a big place either. He lives over on Maple with his girlfriend. Can't miss his place. It's the worst looking trailer on the street."

"Thanks," Mostyn said.

"Mind my asking why you want him?" Reverend Altmeyer said.

"He supposedly saw a yeti or some similar creature,"

Mostyn replied. "Apparently he's become something of a local celebrity."

"Oh, that." The reverend chuckled.

"You don't believe him?" Cashel asked.

"He's a drunk, you know. Hardly a reliable source." Altmeyer's tone was disapproving. "I think he's using the tragedy over at Shiloh to line his pockets."

Mostyn's face indicated he was considering her comment. Then he said, "Thank you for your time, Reverend," and turned to leave.

"Are you with a newspaper?" Altmeyer asked.

Mostyn turned back to look at her. "Government. Health and Human Services," he said, and left. Cashel followed him out the door into the parking lot.

"Rather sad; don't you think, Mostyn?"

"How's that?"

"She's probably in her fifties. Single. And gets put out here to serve a dying parish in a dying town."

"That sums up rural America, Cashel."

"But she's a woman. It's gotta be a sure career killer."

"Oh. Yeah. Probably is. The old boys club, you know. But then we're all equal in Jesus, right?"

"Yeah, right."

They got into the SUV and Mostyn passed the information on to Jones.

"His address is in the file, sir."

"So it is, Jones. So it is."

Jones shook his head, started the vehicle, plugged the address into the GPS, and followed the directions. In a couple minutes, they were parked on the street in front of a gaudy pink derelict. Playing in the front yard were four small children.

Mostyn opened his door. "Cashel, you're with me. The rest of you wait here."

They got out of the vehicle and walked up the drive to the mobile home. A dirty little girl, who may or may not have been kindergarten age intercepted Mostyn and Cashel.

"Who are you?" she asked.

Cashel dropped down to her level. "My name is Arliss, and this man is Pierce. Do you live here?"

The girl nodded.

Arliss continued, "We want to talk to your father. Is he home?"

The girl screwed up her face and looked at Cashel, then Mostyn, and then back to Cashel.

"Is this about the monster?" she asked.

"Yes," Cashel said.

"He's home. It'll cost you to talk to him. He's a cebebity and cebebities get money."

"I see." Cashel said, and stood up. "Will you take us to him?"

"He's inside. Just knock on the door." And she ran off to join the other kids in whatever game they were playing.

"A celebrity." Cashel chuckled. "Maybe the reverend is right."

"Make hay while the sun is shining," Mostyn replied.

As they approached the trailer, Cashel wrinkled her nose. "God. The stench." And when they reached the door she looked at Mostyn.

A smile touched his lips. "Don't want to knock?"

"God." She took a tissue out of her pocket to protect her fingers from the booger encrusted screen door, and knocked.

From somewhere inside, a voice called out, "Who's there?"

Mostyn replied, "We'd like to talk to you about the creature you saw."

In a moment, a man appeared on the other side of the screen door. He was wearing a dirty white T-shirt and a dirty pair of blue jeans. His face had several days worth of stubble on it and his hair was unwashed. A beer bottle was in one hand and the beer belly was evidence he probably wasn't a light drinker. He looked them up and down.

"You want to know about the monster?"

"That's right," Mostyn said.

"It'll cost you."

Mostyn took out his wallet and extracted a fifty dollar bill. He looked over at Cashel. "Can you match this?"

She looked in her purse. "Yes, I can." Out came a twenty, a ten, and four fives, which she turned over to Mostyn.

He said, "A hundred bucks. What's your story?"

The man pushed open the door and held out his hand for the money.

"After we hear your story," Mostyn explained.

Gillies looked momentarily perturbed, but the look quickly passed and a big smile appeared. "Come on in."

Cashel replied, "How about you come out here and show us where it all happened."

"Sure. Sure. I can do that." He opened the screen door and

stepped outside. He was barefoot. He took them around to the back of the mobile home. "Say, I didn't get your names."

"Mostyn. Pierce Mostyn. This is Arliss Cashel."

Gillies wiped off his hand on his grubby jeans. "Pleased to meet you."

Mostyn and Cashel each shook hands with him.

"I suppose you have my name. Obed Gillies. Wife's working. I'm watching the kids." He finished his beer and tossed the bottle towards the back of the yard.

Mostyn nodded his head in confirmation. "You're married?"

"Well, not official like. But we're together and got the kids. You people with the *Times*? Or the *News and Sentinel*?"

"Those local?" Mostyn asked.

"Uh, yeah. *Marietta Times* and *Parkersburg News and Sentinel*. Where you from?"

"Washington, D.C."

He let out a whistle. "I guess I'm hittin' the big time."

Mostyn smiled. "You might say that. Where did you see this creature?"

Obed pointed. "Up there. Back in the hills. I was out lookin' for rabbits or squirrels. Lulinda makes the best stew. Anyway, I lost track of time and it was gettin' dark. So I started headin' back. And that's when I sawed the thing. Caught it in my flashlight beam. Musta been ten feet tall and all hairy and big yeller fangs. I shot at it and it ran away. Although all I had was my twenty-two. Bullet probably jess bounced off that thick black fur."

"You sure it wasn't a bear?" Cashel asked.

"A bear?" Obed let out a laugh. "Oh, that's a good un. I know what a bear looks like and that thing weren't no bear."

"Would you be able to take us up into the hills to where you saw it?" Mostyn asked.

"Uh, I suppose. I mean I'd probably have to find a babysitter and all and they ain't cheap."

"We'll pay you for your trouble." Mostyn told him.

"Oh. Shoot, well in that case, sure. When do you want to go?"

"Tomorrow?" Mostyn said. "Eleven in the morning okay?"

"Sure. That'll be jess fine."

"Then we'll see you tomorrow." Mostyn handed him the hundred dollars and he and Cashel walked back to the SUV.

"You think he'll be sober when we see him tomorrow?" Cashel asked.

"Probably not."

"You believe his story?"

"I believe he saw something. But then Dotty says I believe everything."

Cashel laughed. "She would."

When they got back to the vehicle, the others asked what they'd found out. Mostyn told them what Gillies had said and Cashel provided a description of the door, odor, and Gillies himself.

"I'd say he probably saw something," Mansfield said.

"He's a drunk, Jeffrey." Kemper's voice was filled with

disdain. "He may be out stone cold when we show up tomorrow. Then what?"

"Well, if he is, I have a little something that may solve the problem. The wonders of our modern science that you are so fond of Doctor Kemper."

"I still say we're wasting our time."

"Be that as it may, Dotty," Mostyn said, "I agree with Mansfield. Jones, take Doctor Kemper to Middlebourne so she can commune with the dead, then meet us back here. Call us when you're done, Dotty."

"Will do."

Jones and Kemper left.

"All right, the rest of us will begin canvassing the area," Mostyn said. "We're getting leads on any sightings. Primarily since the Shiloh attack four, no, five days ago now. Let's get to it."

The team members spread out and a long day of door knocking began.

4

BAKER WALKED BACK across West Virginia 2 and down the Heirloom Road. His camera dangled from his neck and sweat rolled down his back. He'd rather be taking a dip in the river than walking along an asphalt road, knocking on doors and talking to people.

The first house he came to only a barking dog replied to his knocking. At the second house, an old woman answered the door. He told her his name, that he was with the Department of Health and Human Services, and with that she closed the door in his face.

Baker walked on to the next place, about five hundred feet down the road, muttering that West Virginia had seceded from Virginia in the Civil War and what was up with all the anti-government sentiment.

At the next place, a woman answered the door. She was probably in her upper twenties and was holding a baby on her hip. A toddler was holding onto her leg.

"Hi, ma'am. My name is Willie Lee Baker." He showed

her his fake ID. "I'm with the Department of Health and Human Services. I'm talking to people about the recent animal attack. Have you ever seen any strange or unusual creatures around?"

"Nope. Never have. But my father-in-law he saw the creature."

"What did it look like?" He got out a notebook and pen.

"He didn't get a real good look, cuz the sun had set and it was jess turnin' dark. But he said a big ol' rock come flying at him, he was driving in an area with lots of trees close to the road, hit the side of his pickup. He stopped, thinkin' it were kids messin' around, and got out. He grabbed his rifle jess to scare 'em, ya know?"

Baker nodded.

"And then another rock come flyin' and smashed in his windshield. He started yellin', my father-in-law that is, and says he marched over towards the trees, when this big hairy thing showed itself. He fired his rifle at it, he says, and the thing disappeared into the trees."

"Did he follow it? Your father-in-law?"

"Heck no. He hightailed it outta there."

"When was this?"

"Oh, lemme see. Maybe a couple months ago."

Baker closed his notebook, thanked her, and moved on to the next house. Which was a bust, as were the next four. House number six, though, gave him some interesting information.

After introductions, Mr. and Mrs. Southwood invited Baker in for iced tea. For which he was grateful, as the heat and humidity were stifling.

"I never saw the thing that some people say they've seen," Mr. Southwood said. "But I think if you want to get to the source of all these rumors, you need to visit the Vander Vrooman place."

"Where's that?" Baker asked, getting out his notebook.

"Easier if I draw you a map," Mr. Southwood said.

"Easy for an outsider to get lost around here," Mrs. Southwood added.

Baker handed Mr. Southwood his notebook, and the old man drew a map and in a few minutes handed the notebook back to Baker.

"Can you follow that, young feller?" Mr. Southwood asked.

"Yes. Looks pretty simple to get to. Why do you think this place is important?"

Mr. Southwood cleared his throat and took a look around, before speaking. "Because those Vander Vroomans just up and disappeared. And it was after that, we started gettin' these murders every now and again."

Mrs. Southwood nodded her confirmation.

"And when was this? That they disappeared?"

"Difficult to say, for sure, as they kept to themselves. But since the War Between the States ended there hasn't been a sighting of them."

"People around here seem to have long memories."

"That they do, young feller. That they do."

"Thank you very much for the information, Mr. and Mrs. Southwood."

Baker finished his iced tea and excused himself.

Walking down the drive he couldn't help but think he'd hit the jackpot.

———

Across town, Pierce Mostyn was knocking on doors. Three so far mentioned they had seen something, but the descriptions were vague. However, most of the people he'd been able to speak to, hadn't seen anything.

He was hot and drained. The heat and humidity were stifling. He came up to a rather nice looking little bungalow. Somewhat better kept than those of it's neighbors. And when he knocked on the door, a girl answered. Mostyn figured she had to be around fifteen.

He gave his name and his spiel about being with the Department of Health and Human Services.

"My ma and pa aren't here. They're at work."

Mostyn noticed she was somewhat flushed and was barely hiding a hicky on her neck. "That's okay. Have they ever talked about seeing a creature around here, or anyone they know that has seen a big hairy creature."

"Uh, no, they haven't. Why do you want to know?"

"Because it might pose a health risk. We need to capture the creature and test it."

"Really?"

Mostyn nodded.

"What kind of health risk?"

"We won't know for sure until we test the creature. Of course, we have to make sure there is a creature to begin with. There seems to be some doubt about that."

"Well, Mike and I saw it."

Mostyn raised his eyebrows. "Whose Mike?"

"My boyfriend."

A slight smile touched Mostyn's lips. That piece of information explained the hicky. "Did you tell your parents?"

"Heck no."

A young man came to the door. "What's going on, Babe?"

"He's from the health department and says that creature we saw might have some disease we could die from."

Mostyn smiled. "I didn't exactly say that. But if you saw the creature, I'd like you to tell me about it." He paused and then added, "I won't tell your parents."

The two kids looked at each other and then the girl said, "Mike and me were out parking. You sure you aren't going to tell my ma and pa?"

"Scouts honor," Mostyn replied.

"Well, like I said, we was out parking and something banged on the roof of the car."

"Scared the shit out of us," Mike volunteered.

"Did you see what it looked like?" Mostyn asked.

"Not at first. It was dark," the girl said.

"We had the windows rolled up and the car was running cuz I had the air on," Mike said.

"Then there was a face pressed up against the glass. And I screamed and it ran away."

"What did the face look like?" Mostyn asked.

"Kind of like a person, but not exactly. And it was wearing what looked like a fur coat."

"Which was weird," Mike said, "because it was a hot night."

"When was this?"

"About three weeks ago." Mike answered.

"Where were you?" Mostyn asked.

The two kids looked at each other. And finally the girl answered. "We were in the parking lot behind the Baptist church. About…"

Mike continued, "Two miles from here. Lots of trees near the church."

"Anything else you can tell me?" Mostyn asked.

The kids shook their heads and the girl once again asked that Mostyn not tell her parents and he said he wouldn't.

Walking down the drive he felt confident they were on to something here that wasn't quite within the realm of normal.

———

Doctor Mansfield wiped his brow with a handkerchief. The heat and humidity were all but unbearable, yet he would bear them. In fact he was positively giddy. He looked over the notes he'd made of his latest interview. Little pieces all fitting together to slowly fill in the puzzle. He was certain that right here in Tyler County was everything he needed to prove his theory. Evolution had indeed reversed itself. All that remained was to secure a specimen.

On the other hand, Doctor Cashel wasn't having much luck. All she could think about was getting back to the hotel and her air conditioned room, taking a shower, and getting a gin and tonic. Perhaps Dotty was right and this was all a lot of hooey. It's just that Mansfield sounded so sure. She sighed. Probably just some kind of weird cult they'd stumbled on. Something the locals or the FBI could handle. No need for the OUP to be involved. Maybe they could head back to DC early. That would be nice. And then her thoughts went back to getting that shower and a really tall gin and tonic.

Special Agent DC Jones didn't spend much time talking to the people in his section of the village. A few had stories to tell, and they were doozies. The rest knew nothing, or were just pulling his leg. If he didn't sense a story in the first thirty seconds, he moved on.

His training and his time in the Bureau had given him a sixth sense when it came to interviewing people. The time spent in the OUP had given him a healthy respect for the stories about things that go bump in the night. He didn't fully understand what Mansfield was excited about, but he had come to a very solid conclusion based on what he was hearing. There was definitely something weird going on here.

5

Kemper and Cashel won and the team ate supper at the Chinese buffet. Over egg rolls, fried rice, Dim Sum, Teriyaki Chicken, wontons, and chow mein, the team discussed the day's events.

"We're dealing with several humans," Kemper declared. "The teethmarks on the bones are sufficient verification. Not to mention the DNA evidence from hair found at the scene. Human."

"Any matches?" Mostyn asked.

"Nothing in the FBI database," Kemper replied, around a bite of egg roll.

"Still mock my 'abhuman', as you put it, theory, Dotty?" Mansfield asked, a smile playing on his lips.

She was undaunted. "No verified occurrences. Might be some weird cult. We should check with Elswick to see if they have any here." She licked her fingers, having finished her egg roll.

And Mansfield was equally undaunted. "Except for

those specimens the government won't even let us examine."

"If they were real abhumans," she countered, "I think Bardon would have been able to get in on the action."

Jones asked, before shoveling in a load of chow mein, "Is there such a thing as reverse evolution?"

Mansfield put his fork down. "Why not? If nature can move in one direction, why can't it move in the other given the right circumstances?"

"I don't know, Doc. You tell me." Jones shoveled in another load of chow mein.

"There's no evidence of devolution. It's nothing more than gothic fiction." Kemper's tone indicated she thought the idea was beyond stupid.

Mansfield favored Kemper with a smile, and turned to Jones. "The human genome is virtually identical to that of our primate cousins. We are basically a hairless bonobo with opposable thumbs. Whatever it was that caused our genome to become different could easily be undone."

"We do have examples of inbreeding leading to deformities and mental deficiency," Baker said.

Cashel shook her head. "Deformities or a proclivity towards disease or lowered intelligence, but no examples of regression as Jeffrey is suggesting."

Mansfield held up his hand. "That we know of. However, I think we must face the reality that we're here due to a fluke of nature. A chance beneficial mutation. And as we all know, most mutations are not beneficial."

Munching on teriyaki chicken, Jones said, "Those Teenage Mutant Ninja Turtles are pretty awesome."

Kemper, Cashel, and Baker burst out laughing. Mostyn shook his head, and said, "Honestly, Jones."

Jones looked confused. "What do you mean?" And that made Kemper, Cashel, and Baker laugh all the harder.

With a wry smile on his face, Mansfield said, "Maybe more like the Incredible Hulk."

"Yeah. He's pretty awesome, too," Jones said, and demolished more teriyaki chicken.

"Comic books and TV shows aside," Mostyn began, "is there any actual evidence for devolution? I mean, we accept evolution but there's no actual proof for that either. We certainly can't reproduce evolution in the lab."

A fork of chow mein paused in midair, and Kemper replied, "You're right, Mostyn, we can't reproduce evolution in the lab. Technically, it's a working hypothesis because it's the best explanation we have for the evidence we see. There is however nothing that indicates devolution has ever existed. Nothing."

"Yet," Mansfield said.

"I can see why Bardon likes you," Kemper replied.

Mostyn changed the subject. "I want to hear what we learned from the locals. Baker?"

"Not much, really. I talked with nineteen people. None of them had seen the creatures, but four of them had friends or relatives who had. I got the names and addresses so we can follow-up. And a couple of people spoke of a haunted house and thought the creatures could be connected to the place. One fellow drew me a map and said we should definitely check the place out."

Mostyn smiled at the mention of the haunted house. "Very good. Cashel?"

"I spoke with twenty-two people. One person saw something about a year ago. Thought it was a wolf or a bear. But the creature didn't act like a wolf or a bear. So he thinks maybe it was whatever is making the attacks."

"Did he get a good look at it?" Mostyn asked.

"No. It was dark and the creature was some distance away. Personally, I'm leaning towards Dotty's thought. Some kind of cult."

"Okay. Thanks. Doc?"

Mansfield cleared his throat, took a sheet of paper out of a pocket, put on his cheaters, and began. "I spoke with eighteen people. Three saw something. All sightings were after sunset, but only one had a fairly good look. He caught the creature in his headlights as it was crossing Highway Two in town."

"Did he describe it?" Mostyn asked.

"Yes. Walked upright. The gait was human, yet not quite. It wore no clothes and was covered with dark colored hair or fur. He caught a glimpse of the face, which he said looked like that of a person."

"How long ago was this?" Mostyn asked.

"April of this year. And for the record, I had three people also mention the haunted house. They told me there was a local legend about a family that lived there which was very reclusive and they just vanished."

"Did you ask where this haunted house is?"

"I did and got directions too."

"Good. Thanks. We'll compare them with Baker's map. Jones?"

He returned his fork to his plate. "I spoke with twenty-three people. Two have relatives who've seen the creature and I got contact information. A fifteen-year-old girl saw a shape outside her window at night. She thought it was somebody trying to look in and screamed. Whatever it was ran off. Her father ran outside, with his shotgun, but didn't see anything. That was about a month ago. Another sighting was by a person out hunting just after sunset, back in January. He saw something he thought was a bear and took a quick shot. He wounded it, because he saw blood, but it ran off. He got scared when he saw the footprints, because they looked human.

"Interesting. Very interesting," Mansfield said. The excitement very apparent in his voice. Kemper merely rolled her eyes.

Jones continued, "Two others got glimpses of something last year. They said they thought what they saw was a person, but not quite. And I had one person, must be about ninety, mention the haunted house and the family that disappeared."

"Good work, Jones." Mostyn paused for a moment to compose his thoughts, then spoke. "I talked with seventeen people, four of whom saw something. The other people I talked to only got vague glimpses." He then related the story the girl and her boyfriend had told him.

Mansfield had a smile on his face. "What do you think, Dotty?"

"Interesting stories. But no proof of anything."

Mansfield pressed. "But this is a growing pile of circumstantial evidence. And when it gets big enough…"

Dotty shrugged. "Then we'll have a big pile of circumstantial evidence. We're scientists, we need concrete proof."

"I agree," Mansfield replied, then he smiled. "There are those creatures the government has under lock and key."

Kemper waved her hand in a dismissive gesture.

"Which means we have a lot of work yet to do," Mostyn said. "So let's finish up here, get some sleep, and get back at it tomorrow."

Mostyn paid for their meals with his OUP provided credit card. They filed out of the restaurant. The night air was warm and muggy. In the distance, coyotes were howling.

"That is such an eerie sound," Cashel said.

Dotty nodded in agreement, and said. "That, at least, is explainable."

6

MOSTYN COULDN'T SLEEP. He got dressed, put his backup revolver in the ankle holster, his semi-automatic in the shoulder holster, and left his room. Down the hall he went to Jones's room. He knocked on the door. No answer. He put his ear to the door and heard faint giggling.

"Shit," he whispered, and took a step away from the door. He walked to Dotty Kemper's room and knocked. No answer. He knocked again.

From inside he heard, "Who is it?"

"Mostyn."

The door opened the length of the chain. "For God's sake, Mostyn, it's one-fifteen. What the hell?"

"I can't sleep. I want to check something out."

"Take Jones."

"He's... Busy."

"Shit. Why me?"

"Because you know how to handle yourself in a situation."

"We have a situation?"

"Not at this moment."

"Oh. You just want to be prepared. All right, I'll be out in a minute."

It was more than a minute, but less than five and Dotty Kemper was in the hall.

"A three-piece suit? What the hell, Mostyn?"

"A blouse and slacks. What the hell, Kemper?"

"Very funny. Where are we going?"

"I want to follow up on something someone I talked to earlier had said."

"Okay. So, where are we going?"

"The Baptist church outside of Heirloom."

"Oh, for Christ's sake."

A smile touched Mostyn's lips. "Maybe it is."

"What?"

"Never mind, Dot. Are you armed?"

"Of course." She touched her fanny pack and pointed to her right ankle.

"Good. Let's go."

They walked to the elevator, took it to the ground floor, and exited the hotel. They walked over to the SUV, and Mostyn pressed the button that unlocked the doors. He got in on the driver's side, Kemper taking the front passenger seat, and in a minute they were driving out of the lot on their way to Heirloom.

"What's so important about the church, Mostyn?"

"It was where one of the sightings took place."

"So why are we going there at this ungodly hour?"

"Couldn't sleep, and got to thinking if lightning might strike twice."

"How lucky for me. I should've followed my first thought and told you to go to hell."

Mostyn sang, "Jesus saves. Jesus saves."

"Sure he does."

"Such a cynic."

"Whatever."

Mostyn chuckled, but said nothing, and in silence they drove the rest of the way to the church.

According to the odometer, Heirloom Baptist church was actually one point six miles outside Heirloom on the Heirloom Road. The small frame building was located fairly close to the road. A drive led around to the back of the building, where Mostyn assumed the parking lot was, based on the description given to him by Mike and his girlfriend.

As he drew near the drive, Mostyn turned off the head-lights. He left the parking lights on until he had turned into the driveway, and then he turned them off as well.

"Why are we going dark?" Kemper asked.

"Least possible disturbance."

"You really think we'll find something?"

"Don't know."

When the big black SUV pulled into the lot, Mostyn and Kemper saw a big old Pontiac a short distance away, not far from the tree line. The car was bouncing, the squeak of the springs just barely audible.

"Looks like someone's going for a ride," Mostyn said.

"Idiots."

"What? You never did that, Kemper?"

"A car? You've got to be kidding?"

"Nope."

"Forget it. Now what?"

Mostyn put the SUV in park and shut off the engine. "Let's go for a walk."

They exited the vehicle, flashlights in hand. The old Pontiac stopped bouncing.

"I guess he scored," Kemper said.

"Hope they don't regret it."

"Now who's the cynic."

"Just saying. Baby's you know."

"Gotta point there, Mostyn."

"This way, Kemper."

Mostyn cut across the lot on a path that would give the occupants of the Pontiac their space. Kemper was next to him. Their flashlight beams illuminated the asphalt, and when the asphalt ended, the short strip of grass before the woods.

Just before the trees, Kemper hesitated. "Awfully dark in there."

"That it is. And there may or may not be a bogeyman in there."

"Yeah, right."

Mostyn and Kemper carefully picked their way into the woods. Behind them, in the east, a golden moon began coming up over the treetops. They heard the Pontiac start and drive out of the lot.

"Bet they're wondering whose SUV that is," Mostyn said.

"Probably scared shitless someone was spying on them and will tell their parents."

Mostyn chuckled. "Probably."

Out of the darkness a rock knocked Kemper's flashlight out of her hand. Mostyn turned his off and they dropped to the ground. All around them they heard grunting and feral sounds. Neither one said a word. Whatever was making the sounds, and there had to be several of them, they were obviously looking for Mostyn and Kemper.

Mostyn touched his pistol to Kemper's hand and then touched her hand with one finger, followed by a second, and then a third.

Kemper wrote "OK" with her finger on Mostyn's hand and pulled her pistol out of the fanny pack.

Mostyn tapped Kemper's hand once, twice, three times. They jumped up, and fired into the darkness.

Several rocks came flying in their direction and Mostyn grunted when one connected with his thigh. And then all was quiet.

Mostyn turned on his flashlight and panned the light and his pistol in a circle around them. Nothing. There was nothing but trees and darkness beyond the flashlight beam.

He squatted down and played the beam of light around until he found Kemper's flashlight. He picked it up and tried the switch.

"Must've broken the bulb."

He heard Kemper say, "Let's go."

He stood and they made their way out of the woods. In the middle of the parking lot, Kemper suddenly stopped.

"What is it, Dot?"

"You know those sounds they were making?"

"A lot of grunts.

"Some were. But most of them…?" She paused, her voice tinged with fear, and turned to face Mostyn.

"Go on."

"They followed the pattern of speech."

7

MOSTYN AND KEMPER decided for the time being they'd keep their adventure to themselves. Although Mostyn did include it in his daily report. So at breakfast they said nothing, although Kemper knew the information would make Mansfield's heart go pitter-patter.

And Obed Gillies was indeed drunker than the proverbial skunk. Mostyn anticipated the possibility, and he and his team showed up early in case they needed to wake him. Lulinda Gillies hadn't yet left for work and was still at home. She wasn't at all happy to see Mostyn.

"So you're the one who gave him all that money so he could get hisself all liquored up."

"I gave him money," Mostyn replied. "But what he did with it was his responsibility. I didn't make him buy booze." Mostyn held out five twenties to her. "You'll probably need this for the children."

She gave him an evil look and snatched the money out of his hand.

"We need to see your husband, Mrs. Gillies." Mostyn said.

She looked him up and down. Looked out to the black SUV full of people. "You're not with no newspaper are you?"

"No, ma'am, we're not." He took out his Health and Human Services ID and showed her.

"What is that? Some kind of police?"

"You might say that. We're trying to understand what we're dealing with here. These animal attacks. If there is a possibility of contagious disease. We need your husband to show us where he saw the creature."

"Good luck with that." Then after a pause, "You believe him?"

"I believe he saw something and I believe it could be dangerous. Beyond just physically killing people."

"I have to go to work and he's supposed to watch the kids."

"Can someone watch them while we're gone?" Mostyn produced another twenty.

"Sure. I'll ask Ellie. He's in the bedroom. If you can get him up, good luck."

Mrs. Gillies picked up the phone, dialed a number, talked with someone, and then hung up. While she was doing that, Mostyn looked around the trailer. About the only thing that could be done with it, in his opinion, was to scrap the thing and get a new one.

"Ellie will be over in a few minutes. She just lives a couple houses down. I gotta go. Will you tell her the money's on the table?"

"I will do that Mrs. Gillies. I'm sorry your husband doesn't take better care of you and the children."

"He was a good man. Still is. Everything changed when he lost his job. Like he lost a part of hisself. Jobs are hard to find around here and a man with no job is like a lost soul. Don't like the coal mining, but at least it was work."

She left. Driving off in an old Chevy Impala that probably should have been in a junkyard somewhere.

Mostyn walked back to the government SUV. "Okay, Jones, you're with me."

Kemper, her voice dripping disdain, said, "He's dead drunk. Isn't he?"

"He is," Mostyn replied.

"As I mentioned yesterday," Mansfield said, "I have something that will help him. I take it with me in case any of my colleagues need something stronger than the traditional hair of the old dog."

"Get your bag, Doc, and come with us."

"What is it?" Kemper asked.

"An enzyme cocktail. A couple scientists at MIT came upon a drunkenness antidote. With funding from the OUP they refined it and now Bardon has it in his arsenal of toys."

"Well, I'll be damned," Kemper muttered. "No more hangovers."

"Righto," Mansfield said, a smile on his face. He retrieved his bag and joined Jones and Mostyn.

The three men entered the trailer just as a small woman approached from down the street.

"I'm Ellie Fitzhugh. Lulinda said you folks was here to talk to that no good husband of hers."

"Yes, we're here to talk to Mr. Gillies," Mostyn said. "You're going to babysit?"

"I am."

"Money's on the table for you," Mostyn said.

He let Ellie Fitzhugh enter the trailer and then he, Jones, and Mansfield followed.

"Bedroom's over that away. Just follow the snoring," Ellie said, pointing the way.

Mostyn nodded his thanks, and walked down the narrow corridor to the room. His companions followed. There, sprawled out on the bed and snoring away, was Obed Gillies.

"Not a pretty picture, Doc," Mostyn said. "You using a hypo? Pills?"

"I have both. Since he's sleeping, I'll give him a shot."

"Have at it," Mostyn replied.

Mansfield squeezed passed Jones and entered the bedroom with Mostyn and Jones behind him.

The doctor opened his black bag, selected a vial and a syringe, took several milliliters of clear fluid out of the vial, and injected it into the snoring Obed Gillies. He didn't even flinch when the needle went in.

"How soon does that stuff work?" Jones asked.

"Fairly quickly," Mansfield answered. "It's like you suddenly have a thousand livers doing detox work on the alcohol."

"Really?" Jones said.

Mansfield nodded.

The three watched Gillies and when his breathing changed slightly, Mansfield informed them he was probably out of his drunken state.

Mostyn shook him and called his name. In a moment the man's eyes flew open.

"What the hell?" he blurted out.

"Did you forget our appointment, Mr. Gillies?" Mostyn asked.

"Oh, yeah, right. You're the fella who wants to see where I saw the monster."

"That's right," Mostyn replied. "These are my associates. Jones and Doctor Mansfield."

"Pleased to meetcha," and Obed stuck out his grubby hand for them to shake, which they did.

"All right, Mr. Gillies, time for you to get dressed and show us where you saw your monster," Mostyn said.

Gillies got out of bed. Near as Mostyn could tell, he was wearing the same grubby T-shirt and jeans he had on yesterday.

"I can go now. You people ready?"

"We're ready," Mostyn said.

Gillies looked the three of them up and down. "You sure ain't dressed to go traipsin' in the woods."

"We'll do fine," Mostyn assured him.

"Okay, then, let's go. We'll have to walk."

Mostyn nodded and the four of them filed out of the trailer.

"Jones, get the others," Mostyn said.

Jones walked over to the SUV, spoke to the other team members, and they got out of the vehicle.

In a minute, seven people were trekking across the hamlet and into the dense forest to the southeast.

8

THE GROUP TREKKED through the forest-covered hills. The tree canopy was so thick and interwoven, there was a certain dusky gloom on the forest floor. Due to the lack of light, there was no undergrowth. Just a thick carpet of decaying leaves, which would have made for fairly easy walking if it weren't for the sometimes steep hills, jutting rock faces, and over all unevenness of the ground.

In an hour of walking, all of them except for Gillies, had fallen or stumbled at least once.

"How much further are we going?" Kemper called out.

"Not much further, ma'am," Gillies replied.

Not much further, however, resulted in another twenty minutes of walking and when they finally arrived at the spot, a GPS reading confirmed Mostyn's suspicion. Gillies had indeed been having a little fun with them.

"Well, here we are!" Gillies was all smiles, and spread his arms wide.

Mostyn looked around.

"This place doesn't look any different than anywhere else we've been in the last hour and a half," Cashel said.

"He's just been leading us in circles," Kemper complained.

"At least I got some really great photos," Baker said, a smile on his face.

"Screw you and your pictures," Kemper shot back.

Baker laughed in reply.

Mostyn himself chuckled. His years of working with Kemper and Baker, had taught him Dotty was a habitual complainer and a natural born skeptic. But under her hard shell she was in fact a loving and kind person. Although if her feelings were hurt, she tended to hold a grudge. Which fact Mostyn now knew from personal experience.

He brought himself back to the task at hand. "To start, Mr. Gillies, where were you and where was the creature you saw?"

Gillies looked around. "I was there, on that rock outcropping."

"Why there?" Mostyn asked.

"It was dark and I needed to get my bearings. If I was up higher, the flashlight would cover more area."

Mostyn, thoughtful, nodded, and said, "Go on. Where was the creature?"

"Well, I shined my light around and that's when I saw what looked like eyes. I swung the light back and that's when I seed the whole thing."

"Where was the creature?" Mostyn asked.

Gillies climbed up the rock outcropping, took a look around, and said, "Over there." He pointed. "By that tree."

"Jones, go stand by the tree Mr. Gillies is indicating."

The special agent walked over to the tree and stood by it.

"Is that where the creature was standing?" Mostyn asked.

"Well, let me see. He ain't as big as the monster. But I think the thing was maybe a little more in the trees."

Jones stepped back a bit. "How's this?" he shouted.

"Yeah, mebbe about there."

"How long was it from when you spotted the creature to when you fired at it?" Mostyn asked.

"Almost right away." Gillies replied. "Jess a couple shots. Didn't want to have to reload, in case it came at me."

"Good thinking," Mostyn said.

A big smile appeared on Gillies's face in response to the complement.

"That's what I thought," he said.

"All right, Mr. Gillies, you can take a break," Mostyn told him. To the others he said, "The rest of us, we start searching from where Jones is standing."

For over an hour, Mostyn and his team searched the area. And in the end, came up pretty much empty-handed. They found three faint partial footprints, a tree that had stopped one of the .22LR bullets, a bit of hair on a tree branch, and a spot of what was possibly blood on a patch of leaf mold.

When the search was over, Mostyn told everyone to take a break while he talked to Gillies.

"After you fired the shots at the creature, Mr. Gillies, what did it do?"

"It took off."

"In which direction?"

"That way." Gillies pointed to the south.

"After the creature left, what did you do?"

"Ran like the devil for home."

"But not by the route you brought us here, did you?"

A sheepish look appeared on his face. "Uh, no, sir."

"I didn't think so. Take us back by the route you took going home that night."

"Yes, sir."

Mostyn rounded everyone up and, with Gillies in the lead, returned to the village of Heirloom. The return trip took half an hour.

Back at Gillies's ramshackle mobile home, Mostyn ordered everyone into the SUV. Then he turned to Gillies.

"I've already given your wife a hundred and twenty dollars."

Gillies blinked.

Mostyn continued, "So I am not giving you any more money."

"Now wait one minute, Mister." Gillies puffed up his chest. "You trying to cheat me?"

"I'm not cheating you at all. I gave that money to your wife."

"Yeah, but *I'm* the celebrity. The money's mine."

"Look, Mr. Gillies, I'm not with a newspaper."

"What do you mean? But you said…"

"I said I was from Washington, D.C. Which is true. I'm

just not with a newspaper. I'm with the federal government."

"The guvmint?"

"That's right."

Gillies spat on the ground. "Shit."

"You and your wife got two hundred and twenty dollars from the American taxpayer. You aren't getting any more."

"That's not fair. You lied to me."

"Mr. Gillies, because of what you saw I could take you to a secret federal facility for further interrogation."

Fear registered on Gillies's face. "But I told you all I knowed."

"However, *I* don't know that for sure. But I'm willing to let it go, if you keep quiet and accept the money I've given you and your wife."

"Uh, sure. Okay. I won't say a word." Then he muttered, almost under his breath, "Don't want to go to no goddam secret guvmint facility."

"Good. Thank you for your time." Mostyn turned away and started for the SUV, stopped, and turned back to look at Gillies. "And Mr. Gillies?"

"Yes, sir?"

"You have a good wife. Treat her and your children well."

"Uh, yes, sir. I shore will, sir."

"If you don't, I have ways of finding out."

Gillies didn't say anything, but even at that distance he could see the fear on the man's face.

Mostyn gave him a lazy salute, said, "Goodbye," and joined his team in the SUV.

"What's next, Boss?" Jones asked.

Mostyn thought a minute before speaking. "We need to talk to the people at Shiloh and take a look at this haunted house people are talking about."

"There are hundreds of abandoned houses and buildings, Mostyn," Kemper said, her voice dripping sarcasm. "Maybe we should call in the Ghostbusters."

Mostyn smiled. "No need. That's why we're here."

9

THE MORNING SUN was bright and hot. The air, clammy and heavy. The hotel clerk told Mostyn, when he walked by, that they were in for a big thunderstorm. Mostyn thanked him for the information.

Yesterday afternoon, Mostyn and his team went back and talked with the people who'd mentioned the haunted house and the local lore about the family that had disappeared. All were in agreement as to the house's location, confirming the information on the map Mr. Southwood had drawn for Baker, and that the family had last been seen "sometime after the War Between the States".

From the directions he'd received on how to get to the place, he put the house a couple miles to the south of Heirloom in an area of dense woods and no access roads.

"Oh, thar once was a road," an old-timer had told Mostyn. "But I don't think it's been used in over a hunnert years. You might find some trace of it. But I doubt it." And he'd punctuated his last sentence with a long spit of brown tobacco juice. Cashel had to turn away, afraid she might throw up her lunch.

The first stop, however, this morning was the little unincorporated hamlet of Shiloh, scene of the recent mass murders. Jones drove the big black SUV south-southwest along the winding country roads to the hamlet, situated on the southwest bank of Middle Island Creek.

"We're out in the middle of God-forsaken nowhere," Kemper said, when she got out of the vehicle.

Cashel laughed. "This is West Virginia, Dotty. It's a beautiful little island of natural wonder. Just enjoy it."

"She's a city gal," Mostyn said. "Get's the hives when there's too much greenery."

Dotty merely said, "Shut up, Mostyn", and directed her attention to the houses that made up the place.

"The forest is right there," Baker said, pointing to the wall of trees just to the south of the houses.

Jones added, "Be real easy to sneak up on the place."

"That's what I was thinking," Baker said, as he snapped a few pictures of the area.

"Okay, people, let's talk to these folks. Shouldn't take us long," Mostyn said.

The team spread out and commenced door knocking.

———

An hour later they were back on the road. They'd talked with the survivors, who unfortunately couldn't tell them much. The attack had taken place late at night and in the middle of a severe thunderstorm.

"The thunder was so loud and intense, it was like the artillery barrages we used to lay down on the Taliban. Couldn't hear a damn thing," one person told Baker.

Mostyn found the person who'd seen the creatures coming out of the trees.

"I'd just found Willy, my dog, when a bolt of lightning lit up everything, just like it was noon. And that's when I saw them. Coming out of the woods. I hightailed it on home, locked the doors, got out my twelve-gauge, and loaded it with double-aught buck. Those poor families. They never had a chance."

"Why's that?" Mostyn asked.

"They didn't believe in guns. Pacifists. Came here from Baltimore, I think, some ten years ago. Back-to-the-land types." He was quiet for a few moments before he asked, "Do you know what those things are?"

"No, I don't, Mr. Divers, that's why I'm here. To find out what they are and to stop them."

Divers said nothing. Merely nodded his head. Mostyn bid him a good day and left.

Jones, at the wheel of the big SUV, guided it expertly along the winding road. When a straight stretch of highway appeared, he said, "You know, Boss, that haunted house people keep bringing up is about halfway between Heirloom and Shiloh."

"Okay, go on."

"Well, remember Gillies's statement that the beast went south after he shot it?"

"Yes."

"And at Shiloh the things came out of the woods which

are south of the village. But what if they did that to avoid crossing the open area north of the village?"

Mostyn nodded. "I see where you're going. Good thinking, Jones."

"Maybe we ought to talk to the sheriff and see if the house is the central point for all of the attacks."

"You just earned your paycheck, Jones. Let's go pay Elswick a visit."

10

INCREDULITY WAS all over Sheriff Elswick's face. "You're serious?"

"I am," Mostyn answered plainly.

The sheriff raised his eyebrows. "I heard the stories. Checked out the place myself. Nothing there. Just talk. Some of these people are so superstitious they're afraid of their own shadow."

Mostyn favored Elswick with his best poker face. "That may be, Sheriff. Nevertheless, what you've shown me is that the haunted house is in the center of most of the recent attacks. I and my people would like to take a look at the place."

The sheriff leaned back in his chair, pushed out his lips, and studied Mostyn. Finally, he leaned forward. "Okay. I'll send Deputy Ohse with you. The place is difficult to get to and I don't want y'all getting lost."

"Thank you, Sheriff."

"A wild goose chase, if you ask me. But then you weren't really asking, were you?"

"No, I wasn't."

Mostyn and his team walked back out to where their SUV was parked in the front of the building. In a moment a Tyler County squad car pulled up, and the man behind the wheel introduced himself as Derek Ohse, and indicated they were to follow him. Mostyn and the others piled into the SUV and Jones started the vehicle. Ohse gunned the big old Ford Police Cruiser, and Jones, a smile on his face, pulled his sunglasses down from the top of his head, and accepted the challenge of keeping up with the deputy.

At speeds that were more at home on the Daytona Speedway than the highway, the Police Cruiser and the big SUV wound their way around the West Virginia hill country. At one point, the SUV slid over onto the gravel shoulder.

Cashel screamed. Kemper cursed loudly. Baker and Mansfield were white knuckled, holding on to whatever they could to avoid being thrown about.

Mostyn looked over at Jones, his tone was matter of fact. "You think you can at least try to keep us on the road?"

Back on the pavement, Jones grinned. "Your wish is my command, sir."

When the Police Cruiser finally pulled over along a desolate stretch of county road, Kemper breathed a sigh of relief. "Finally," she muttered.

"Really," Cashel said, in agreement.

Jones chuckled and turned around. "Got us here in one piece. Top in my class on the driving course."

Kemper gave him the finger and said, "Shit."

There was a knock on Jones's window. He pressed the button and the window slid down.

A big smile appeared on the deputy's face, and he extended his hand to Jones. "Mighty fine driving there. Didn't think this tank could do it."

"DC Jones." And Jones shook hands with the deputy.

"Everybody out," Mostyn said.

Once everyone was out of the SUV, and introductions performed, Mostyn told his people to grab whatever equipment they might need. Especially firearms and flashlights. He then invited the deputy to lead on.

"We have quite a hike," Ohse informed them. "There once was a road that led up to the place and you can find remnants of it in spots. For the most part, though, it's gone."

"How far?" Kemper asked.

"The place is up on the peak. And that's something over a thousand foot elevation. Plus we have dense forest, gullies, and you name it to get through to get there. Take us at least an hour."

Kemper didn't thank him for the information; she just muttered, "Shit," put her hands on her hips, and shook her head in disbelief.

The forest was indeed dense. The tree canopy was so thick it effectively eliminated the sun and cast the forest floor in a Stygian gloom. Which made it very easy to trip over fallen tree branches, rocks, and any other snag nature thought to put in the way.

Mansfield said, "It's so quiet. No birds. No animals. Nothing."

"Noticed that when I was out here before," Ohse replied. "No wonder folks get the heebie-jeebies. The old-timers say the Vander Vrooman family is still here."

"You mean like ghosts?" Baker asked.

Ohse smiled. "No. As in still actually here."

"How can that be?" Kemper asked.

"Abhumans," Mansfield blurted out.

"Ab what?" Ohse asked.

"Abhumans, Deputy. Human beings who have regressed back to an animal state on a genetic level."

"Well, if you mean the Vander Vroomans became monsters, beasts, then that's what some of the old timers believe."

Mansfield was overjoyed. "Yes! I knew it."

"What do the others believe?" Kemper asked.

Ohse laughed. "The others think the family was cursed and that's why they left New York and came here. And...," he paused for effect before continuing, "they never die. Instead, they turn into ghouls."

Kemper shook her head. "Inbred morons," she muttered.

"That's not very PC, Doctor Kemper," Cashel said.

"Ask me if I give a flying fuck," Kemper shot back.

Mostyn interrupted. "Mission, people." To Ohse, he said, "Do you have any unsolved cases similar to what you're encountering now?"

"Don't have anything in detail, really, prior to the Second World War. And then mostly missing persons."

"Did the people go missing mostly in this area?" Mostyn pressed.

"Don't rightly know. We can take a look when we get back."

"And from the World War until now?" Mostyn asked.

"That's when we start seeing what was put down to random animal attacks."

"In this area?"

"Yeah. From the river south just passed Shiloh. And from Arvilla to southeast of Sistersville."

"Anything in Middlebourne?"

"No. Seem to mostly have occurred in the forest or the unincorporateds," Ohse answered.

"When we get back, I'd like to see where these disappearances and animal killings took place on a map."

"Sure, Agent Mostyn. We can do that."

The going was not easy through the forest. And the deathly silence got on everyone's nerves. Although Mansfield seemed the most buoyant and upbeat. Perhaps spurred on by his hope to find specimens of true abhumans.

Climbing out of a ravine, Kemper declared, "If I have to drag myself out of one more muddy, messy, godforsaken ravine, I'm going to shoot somebody."

Ohse called back, "Thank the Lord I'm not going to have to arrest you." He helped her up the last few feet and got her on level ground. Pointing, he said, "There it is. The Vander Vrooman place."

In an overgrown clearing stood a sprawling three-story house. Paint long gone, the wood was weathered a dark gray.

Cashel said, "Rather unheard of to see a Dutch Colonial home in three stories."

"And with so many additions and wings," Mansfield added.

"Apparently a work in progress," Cashel replied. "Adding on as the family grew."

"Makes sense," Mansfield said.

Surrounding the place was a four foot high wall made of stone.

"That wall isn't high enough to keep out much other than small animals," Jones observed.

"Maybe it was more for decoration," Kemper said. "You know, this is our land and here is a pretty wall to make you aware of it."

"As good an explanation as any," Mostyn said.

They walked across the overgrown field, Ohse in the lead, through what once may have been garden plots for the family. As they came upon an opening in the wall, where a gate had once been, they spied a one-story barn falling in on itself on the other side of the house.

The drive, once gravel, no longer crunched underfoot; so overgrown it was. They followed the circle of the driveway around to the door, which was partway open.

"Looks like we can make ourselves at home," Jones said.

"Not much home to make," Ohse replied. "Pretty much all of the stuffed furniture has rotted away. No carpet.

Otherwise that would have been gone too. There are remnants of some rugs."

The group made its way into the Vander Vrooman mansion, flashlights on to illuminate the darkness.

"God, is that animal shit I'm walking on?" Cashel blurted out.

"That and bones and nesting material and who knows what else," Ohse explained. "The upper floors aren't as bad."

"Maybe we can open the shutters?" Kemper suggested.

"Good idea," Baker said.

The front door opened directly into a large room, which appeared to take up the front half of the main floor of the original house. On either side of the door were two windows and on each end there was one window and a large stone fireplace.

When the interior shutters were opened, light poured in through the windows. What everyone saw was a ruin of what was once a beautiful room. The rotting and moldering remains of the sofas and chairs dotted the room. None were usable. The floor was indeed littered with all manner of refuse. Animal droppings, bones, leaves, twigs, and other remains no longer identifiable.

Jones kicked aside some of the litter. "Huh. Look at that. Hardwood floors."

"Probably too expensive to bring carpeting from out east," Baker said.

"Okay, people, listen up," Mostyn said. "Kemper, Cashel, take the third floor. Jones, Mansfield, the second.

Baker, you're with me. We'll see what's here on the main floor."

"I'll go with the ladies," Ohse volunteered. "There is a cellar too. Two levels, actually."

"Thanks," Mostyn said.

Everyone moved out to their search areas. Mostyn and Baker walked from the front room into the hallway that led to the rooms at the back of the house, and which contained the stairway to the upper levels.

The dining room was off the hallway, between the kitchen and the front room. Baker went to work with his camera. The dining room table was littered with dishes and the remains of some long past meal. Into the kitchen they went. The story was the same.

"No meals have been prepared here for some time," Baker said, as he took a picture.

From the main hall, a side hall took the OUP agents into the other rooms of the house. None showed any signs of recent occupancy, save perhaps by common woodland animals. But even traces of them were few.

When all the rooms had been searched, Mostyn and Baker returned to the front room. Having preceded them were the others, for the upper floors were smaller.

"Find anything of interest?" Mostyn asked.

"Not on our floor," Mansfield said.

Jones added, "Just bedrooms and they haven't been used in ages."

"Same on our floor," Kemper said. "The roof is leaking in quite a few spots. I'm surprised the place is still standing."

"Nothing on the main floor either," Mostyn informed the rest of his people. He looked at Ohse. "Where's the cellar entrance?"

"Outside."

"Let's take a look."

Ohse was out the front door and said over his shoulder, "It's over here."

Mostyn and his people filed out of the front door, following the deputy, who took them around to the side of the house.

"As you can see, there used to be doors covering the entrance. They rotted away some time ago," Ohse said.

For a moment they all stood looking at the opening, with stairs that descended into the dark. Then Mostyn started down the stairs, flashlight in hand. The others followed. When he reached the bottom, he played the beam of light around the room. The rest of his team followed suit.

Here, the floor was hard-packed earth. There was evidence of animal activity, however no animals were around. Wooden bins and shelves in various stages of decay, held the remains of foodstuffs laid up for some long ago winter.

Mostyn turned to Ohse. "You said there's a second level?"

"Right. Over here."

The deputy led them through another room that was similar to the first and had at one time probably been where hams and game were hung. On the far side of the room was a doorway and stone steps that descended into a room that formed a sub-basement. The group entered the lower room.

"Wonder why they'd have something like this?" Cashel asked.

The room was littered with tables, chairs, broken lamps, and other discarded items.

"This is the dump," Jones said.

"Certainly looks like it," Kemper added.

Ohse corrected them. "The real dump is in the woods. This stuff is here because they probably thought they might be able to fix it or repurpose it."

At the far end was a short door and Mostyn asked Ohse where it went.

"Don't know if it goes anywhere. Won't open. And hasn't been opened for a very long time. We didn't pursue trying to open it because of its obvious lack of use. Besides, there's no evidence anyone's been out here in a hundred or more years. No sign of squatters and not even the local pranksters come out here."

Mostyn said nothing. His thoughts, however, drifted off to indictments of sloppy investigative work.

"Any tools around here?" he asked.

"Tool shed by the barn," Ohse replied.

"Jones, go with the deputy, here, and find something to take this door down."

"Yes, sir," Jones said, and started walking back to the cellar entrance.

"You think something's behind it?" Ohse asked.

"Won't know until we look," Mostyn answered.

The deputy shrugged his shoulders and went in pursuit of Jones.

When he was gone, Kemper said, "Talk about a bunch of laid back hillbillies. There's a door and they can't be bothered to find out what's on the other side. Could be the skeletons of all those missing people."

"You'd love that, wouldn't you?" Mostyn said.

"Damn right I would. It'd make my little forensic anthropologist heart go pitter-patter."

Mostyn and the rest of his team looked over the pile of junk, Cashel finding a brass and porcelain oil lamp.

"Wow!" she began. "This is nice. Clean up the brass and get a chimney for it. Look really nice on my end table."

"Take it," Mostyn said.

"Really?"

"Sure. I don't think the owners will come after you."

"Gee, thanks, Mostyn."

He smiled in response.

Jones and Ohse returned, bringing with them an axe, adze, and a crowbar. "This ought to get us through the door," Jones said, with a look on his face indicating he was very proud of himself.

"Have at it, then, Paul Bunyan," Mostyn told him.

Jones shed his suit coat, made a big show of spitting on his hands and rubbing them together. With a big smile on his face, he grabbed the axe and gave it a mighty swing. There was a loud thunk as the axe head sank into the wood. He wiggled it free and swung again.

"Concentrate on the hinges," Mostyn said.

"Good idea, Boss." Jones took another swing, redirecting it towards the door's hinges.

After half an hour, the four hinges holding the door to its substantial frame were demolished. Nevertheless it remained in place.

"Must be barred on the other side," Ohse said.

"That's an odd place to bar a door, isn't it?" Baker asked.

Ohse shrugged. "I guess so."

Mostyn directed Jones to use the adze to remove the wood bars holding the planks together and then the crowbar to pry the planks apart.

Jones wiped his brow. "Gotcha, Boss." He went to work on the door and in another hour it lay demolished on the floor. A large beam on the other side of the lintel lay across the top three stone steps.

Mostyn turned on his flashlight and shined the beam of light into the opening. The steps descended into the darkness.

"Well, Ohse, what do you make of that?" Mostyn asked.

The deputy peered into the gloom the flashlight created. "They seem to go down a long way."

Mostyn addressed the group. "Jones and Ohse will come with me to see where the stairs end up. The rest of you stay here."

With flashlight in one hand and pistol in the other, Mostyn went down the steps, followed by Jones and Ohse. When they at last reached the bottom, Jones quipped, "Thought they'd never end. Was beginning to think I'd bypassed the Grim Reaper and gone straight to hell."

"Might still prove true," Mostyn said.

"Counted one hundred and ninety-eight steps," Ohse informed them.

"At least there aren't any pics of frogs fucking chicks with big tits," Jones said.

Mostyn smiled. "Miss that, do you?"

Jones let out a derisive laugh. "Hell no. Well, the chicks yeah. The frogs, no."

Ohse asked, "Frogs fucking chicks? What's that all about?"

Jones said, "I'll tell you about it later. Got captured underground by a bunch of subterranean degenerates. A whole city of them. Only good thing was that they sure were into fucking—"

"Jones." Mostyn's tone was sharp. "Classified. And mind on business at hand."

"Yes, sir." To Ohse, Jones said. "I didn't tell you anything. That was just a bad dream caused by drinking too many tequila shots."

"What are you guys into?" Ohse asked. "I thought you people were with Human Services."

"We are," Mostyn lied. "Our work is mostly classified. We'll follow this tunnel for a little bit to see if it takes us anywhere."

The tunnel was on the narrow side, barely allowing two average size men to stand next to each other. Mostyn, Jones, and Ohse walked single file. Three hundred feet into the tunnel the first side branches appeared.

"Okay, guys," Mostyn began, "I think we go back. Don't want to get lost down here."

"Sounds good to me," Ohse said.

"Whoa! What the hell?"

"What is it, Jones?" Mostyn asked.

"Down that branch. I could've sworn I saw something shining. Like eyes."

Mostyn and Ohse added their flashlights to Jones's, but there was nothing to see.

"I know I saw something," Jones said, his voice insistent. He took a couple dozen steps into the passage and squatted. "Hey guys! Look!"

Mostyn and Ohse joined him. There, in their flashlight beams, was the faint imprint of a foot in the dust and crumbled surface of the hard-packed dirt floor. A human foot, with markings as if it had claws.

11

JONES STOOD. "I think this is the part in the movie where they say, 'Oh, shit'."

"I think you're right, Jones," Mostyn said. "Let's go back."

They trotted out to the main tunnel and retraced their steps. When they reached the stairs, they ran up two at a time. Once in the sub-basement, Mostyn paused a moment to catch his breath, and then ordered everyone to find any glass they could.

"There are a bunch of old canning jars in the other room," Kemper said.

"Good. Get them," Mostyn said, his voice tense.

"What is it?" Kemper asked.

"Think K'n-yan," he replied.

Her eyes grew big and round. "Oh, shit."

"Come on, people," Mostyn called out. "Follow Dotty and be quick about it."

They rounded up a couple dozen jars filled with food

preserved perhaps a hundred or more years ago.

Mostyn took a couple jars and smashed them a dozen steps down, backed up a couple steps, took the jars Kemper handed him and smashed them. The odor of rotten preserves mingled with the musty air.

"Just the smell ought to deter anything down there," Ohse said.

When the top dozen steps were littered with glass, Kemper and Cashel broke the remaining jars in a wide semi-circle around the entrance to the tunnels below.

"Hopefully that will be a sufficient deterrent," Mostyn said. "Now let's get us some reinforcements."

The group made their way out of the cellar and when above ground took a look at the pitch black sky. Lightning flashed and a few seconds later the thunder boom was so loud the ground shook.

"I don't think we're going anywhere," Ohse said.

"Afraid to drive in a little rain?" Jones taunted

"This isn't going to be just a little rain," Ohse replied.

Large drops began falling and then hail the size of walnuts began bouncing off the ground.

"You're right, Ohse," Mostyn said. "Into the house."

Lightning flashed and the thunder boomed loudly. The drops of rain fell with greater frequency and intensity and the hail began to fall by bucketfuls. They ran to the house, pelted by rain and hail.

"Didn't think I'd be glad to be back in here," Jones said

Thunder boomed and the house shook.

"God, that was close," Kemper said.

Cashel set her lamp down in a corner. "Think we can build a fire?" she asked.

"I wouldn't," Ohse said. "Chimneys are probably full of stuff. Haven't been cleaned since forever."

The house shook again and the boom was so loud, hands instinctively went to ears to cover them.

"Are the thunderstorms always this intense?" Kemper asked.

The house shook again in response to the thunder.

"Not always," Ohse said. "Seems to be worse the higher up you go."

All of a sudden the wind picked up, hurling rain and the last of the hail against the windows. Several of the old panes broke.

"Best to close the shutters," Ohse said.

Flashlights went on, while Jones, Mansfield, and the deputy closed the shutters to keep the weather out.

"Let's clear a spot and bring in some chairs," Mostyn said, as he used his feet to push debris into a pile.

"How long is this going to last?" Baker asked.

Ohse shrugged. "Could end quickly. Could go on for hours."

"Damn," Kemper muttered.

"What?" Mostyn asked.

"No cellphone reception."

"Hopefully we won't need it," Mostyn replied.

Visible through the cracks and crevices in the shutters and around the door was a brilliant flash of lightning; and, when the thunder boomed just after the flash, the house again shook on its foundation.

Cashel found a broom in the kitchen, and with the help of a couple small ash shovels, a spot was cleared and made relatively free of debris. Mansfield, Jones, and Ohse found enough wooden chairs in the dining room for everyone. They formed a circle and everyone sat looking at each other, while outside the storm howled.

"So what exactly did you guys see down there?" Kemper asked.

"Tunnels," Mostyn said.

"Maybe pretty extensive," Jones added.

"And…?" Kemper prompted.

"I thought I saw a pair of eyes in my flashlight beam," Jones said. "But when we saw the footprint, that confirmed it."

"Footprint?" Cashel said.

Jones nodded. "Human, but with indications of claws on the ends of the toes."

"Good God," Kemper muttered.

Mansfield was all smiles and rubbed his hands together. "Yes! We must find these beings and capture some specimens for study."

Ohse, though, was agitated. "If whatever is down there is killing people, it needs to be destroyed."

"Now, Deputy," Mansfield began, "I can understand—"

Ohse cut the doctor off. "No, I don't think you do. You aren't from around here. These aren't your people getting killed. To you, this is, what, like some kind of zoo animal."

"Look, Ohse, we want to get to the bottom of this," Mostyn soothed, "just like you. The most important thing is to stop the threat. Everything else is number two. And since I am in charge, that's what we'll be doing. Understand?"

Ohse nodded, although the anger still showed on his face.

However, Mansfield was now upset. "Look here, Mostyn, this just might be the most important find since evolution was first advanced as a viable explanation of human origins. Now we see evidence of human degeneration. Reverse evolution. Surely—"

Mostyn held up his hand. "The first order of business is to protect these people here, in this State. Once that's done, then we can pursue your evidence. Understand?"

Mansfield didn't say anything.

Mostyn repeated, "Doctor Mansfield, do you understand?"

Mansfield looked Mostyn in the eyes. "I understand."

"Good."

Another thunder boom shook the house to its foundation. Mansfield stood and walked down the hall towards the kitchen.

"He's really hellbent on this… What's it called?" Jones said.

"Abhumans," Kemper answered. "The idea of human regression, physically and mentally, to something less than human." She stood. "I'll see if he's all right." And walked out to the kitchen.

The wind continued to howl, the panes of window glass rattled, the shutters shook, and even the door jumped in it's frame.

Cashel looked around the room. "I hope this place holds together."

"It should," Ohse said. "It's built like a fort."

Kemper and Mansfield returned. He sat, but Kemper walked over to one of the fireplaces.

"Why is this abhuman thing so important to you, Jeffrey?" Cashel asked.

Mansfield took a deep breath. "I guess it's a question of metaphysics. The nature of being. We wrestle with the concepts of good and evil. Especially evil. Why do we humans behave so badly when we want to be good?"

"I guess everyone asks that question," Cashel said.

"Precisely," Mansfield said.

From the other side of the room, Kemper said, "And if God is good, why is there so much evil?"

"Right again," Mansfield said. "So the question is asked, 'What are we?' If we are angels, why do we act like devils? If we are basically good, why do we do — and even seem to relish — what's bad? Does being human mean we're above the animals? Or does being human mean we're really beasts with a mask of civility?"

"Any answers?" Mostyn asked.

Mansfield rubbed his hands together and his face glowed with excitement. "Evolution posits a one-way progression from the simple to the complex. Humans, along with all other primates, had a common origin. Along the way, nature's various experiments didn't all make it. Not every primate, human or otherwise, survived. So one could say, nature itself tends to prune the bush leaving only the most desirable branches."

"So far nothing new here," Mostyn said.

"Precisely. But the theory of evolution operates under the assumption that life always moves from simple to complex. In other words, a closed system. But no system is truly closed. We see this in the second law of thermodynamics. The conversion of energy from one form to another is not perfect. There is waste. Heat.

"So what if the development of species, the progression, is also accompanied by regression? Wasted energy, as it were. Entropy, this wasted energy, increases the randomness of the universe. Makes it less orderly. I see evolutionary regression as the result of entropy in the evolutionary process."

"But where's the proof?" Kemper asked.

Mansfield smiled. "It just may be in the tunnels beneath this house."

Lightning flashed, thunder boomed, and the wind shrieked. The front door blew in and a set of shutters flew open, rain and glass blowing in. Jones jumped up to secure the shutters and Ohse dashed to the door.

There was a choked off cry of alarm, and then Deputy Ohse sank to his knees and pitched over onto his back. The lightning flashed and everyone could see his face was gone. It had been chewed off.

12

"OH, MY GOD!" Cashel screamed.

Mostyn dashed to the door, his pistol drawn, but nothing was there. He closed the heavy door. "Jones, Baker, bring some of that ruined furniture here to block the door."

While Jones and Baker were wrestling with a ruined sofa, Mostyn dragged the body of the dead deputy out of the way. The two men pushed the decayed sofa against the door.

Mostyn nodded his approval. "That ought to slow down whatever's out there."

"What about the windows?" Cashel asked, her voice tense and jittery.

"You have your firearm?" Mostyn asked her.

She nodded.

"Then use it, if you have to."

The word "okay" was barely audible.

"Listen up, people," Mostyn began, "whatever these

things are, they're deadly. Don't be a hero and don't be afraid to use your firearm."

"We really need to capture one of these creatures," Mansfield said.

"You know, Doc," Baker began, "I've been on a lot of missions and taken a lot of pictures. Sometimes, as much as I'd have wanted to have it otherwise, the camera had to be set aside in favor of a gun or some other weapon. Survival had to take the place of science. Something to think about."

The look on Mansfield's face indicated it wasn't something he wanted to think about.

Lightning flashed and after a few moments the thunder boomed, less loudly than before.

"Storm's moving off," Mansfield said.

"Good," was Mostyn's reply.

"The sooner we're out of here, the better," Cashel said.

More thunder rumbled and it sounded soft and distant. Mostyn opened the shutters on one of the windows and looked out on the open area surrounding the house. "Rain's letting up and most of the hail has melted. Jones, I want you to escort Kemper and Cashel to the SUV. Drive to wherever you need to go to get a cell-phone signal. First, call in our situation to Bardon. Request back-up and tell him it's urgent. We need it before Sheriff Elswick gets a crusade together to avenge Ohse's death. Let some time pass and then call Elswick and report his deputy's death."

"Got it, Boss."

"Baker, Mansfield, and I will stay here to protect the

body. You only come back when Elswick arrives. Kemper, Cashel, you stay with the vehicle."

"Like hell, Mostyn," Kemper said. "I want in on this. If these things truly are abhumans, then this is a real find. In fact, I'm staying. I'm not going anywhere."

Doctor Mansfield was all smiles.

Mostyn looked at the floor. "Dotty."

"Don't 'Dotty' me, Mostyn. I don't need protecting."

"Very well, Dot." He turned to Jones and Cashel. "You two okay by yourselves?"

Jones waved his hand, dismissing Mostyn's concern. "Don't worry, Boss. I got this."

Cashel was hesitant, but after a moment she said, "Jones and I will be fine, Mostyn."

"Best leave now, then, before it gets dark."

Jones and Baker moved the decayed sofa blocking the door and when it was out of the way, Jones, pistol ready, opened the door. However, no monster appeared. Only a soft rain. He and Cashel left, she carrying her lamp under her arm. Mostyn and the others watched until they disappeared into the forest.

————

The sun had just set when the whump-whump of the big Chinook was heard.

"Sounds like the cavalry has just crested the hill," Mostyn said.

Baker, who was stretched out over four chairs, lazily sat up. "Good. Maybe they'll let us go home."

Kemper's tone was derisive. "How long have you worked for the OUP?"

"Yeah, well, a guy can hope. Can't he?" Baker replied, a smile on his lips.

Mostyn went to the door and opened it. The big Chinook was trying to find a place to land. With a sixty-foot rotor diameter, the task was proving to be a challenge due to the trees that dotted the open area surrounding the house.

Baker, Kemper, and Mansfield joined Mostyn just outside the front door. They watched the big chopper hover about forty feet in the air, its floodlights illuminating the ground below. The side cargo door opened and two lines were dropped. Men dressed in black abseiled to the ground. Other men in the helicopter prepared a bundle of equipment and lowered it to their compatriots. The first load was followed by a second and a third. The final pieces of equipment were three robots, lowered one by one to the ground. The robots were followed by more men in black. When the last one had joined the formation, the lines were hauled in and the Chinook flew off.

Mostyn and his team walked over to the twenty new arrivals, who had broken formation and were busy sorting out the equipment. One of the men separated himself and trotted over to meet Mostyn and his people halfway.

Looking from Mostyn to Baker to Mansfield, he asked, "Special Agent in Charge Mostyn?"

"I'm Mostyn."

"Captain Ronald Pittman, OUP Special Forces."

Mostyn and the captain shook hands. Mostyn then introduced him to the other members of his team.

"What can you tell me about the situation?" Pittman asked.

Mostyn gave him a thumbnail sketch of what had happened since their arrival at the dilapidated mansion.

"The indications, then, are that these creatures live underground, is that it?" Pittman asked.

"That's our working hypothesis," Mostyn replied. "The Martense family in the Catskills, according to an unverified report, had taken to living underground. We're of the same opinion that's what's happened here."

"And this based on the eyes Special Agent Jones said he saw and the footprint three of you saw."

"Correct," Mostyn confirmed.

"How do we get to the tunnels?"

Flashlights appeared at the tree line. Mostyn counted sixteen of them and in a moment, they were crossing the open area. Captain Pittman turned in the direction of Mostyn's gaze.

"Who're they?" he asked.

"I'd say that's the local authority about to claim jurisdiction," Kemper said.

Mostyn smiled. "Yep. That's what I'd say, too."

Pittman growled and uttered the word, "shit", and then shook his head. "That's all we need. Damn locals."

"Let me talk to the sheriff," Mostyn said.

"Go ahead," Pittman replied. "We'll get our equipment in position." He started walking back to where his men were standing.

"I'll show you the entrance to the cellars," Mansfield volunteered.

"Thanks," Pittman called over his shoulder.

Mostyn met Sheriff Elswick's party as they were coming through the opening in the wall where the gate had been.

"Who are those people, Mostyn?" Elswick demanded, his tone indicating he wasn't in a good mood.

"Health and Human Services Special Forces."

"Yeah, right. And I'm the president." To his men, Elswick said, "Tyler, Dempsey, secure Ohse's body. The rest of you, get down to that cellar."

While the Sheriff was directing his men, Jones stepped to Mostyn's side and told him Cashel was with the vehicle.

Elswick turned his attention back to Mostyn. "I don't know who you are or who you're really with, and I don't care. This is *my* county and *I'm* in charge. You take orders from me, or leave. That's your choice."

To Mostyn, Jones said, "I brought the LORSCOM."

"Thanks, Jones. Set it up and get Bardon."

"Right, Boss." Jones, with a large black case in hand, set off towards the house.

"What's he doing?" Elswick asked.

"With cellphone reception non-existent here, Jones brought our Long-Range Satellite Communicator. He's going to talk to our boss."

"You do that, Mostyn. Now if you'll excuse me." Elswick strode off in the direction of the house, and waved for his men to join him.

Mostyn followed, and matched Elswick's stride. "Look, Sheriff, we should work together on this."

"Fine. I agree. Put your men under my command."

"That's not what I meant."

Elswick stopped. His men continued on towards the mansion. "Of course it isn't. Look, Mostyn, I know how you goddamn Feds operate. Joint operation. Shit. You fucking takeover and leave us hayseeds and country yokels twiddling our thumbs. Well, not in *my* county. You hear me?"

"I hear you, Elswick. And I'm here to tell you I'm not like that."

"Says you. Tell your men to back off."

Up ahead Captain Pittman and his man were in a standoff with Sheriff Elswick's. Both sides had firearms aimed at the other.

Elswick ran over to join his men.

Mostyn shook his head. "This is crazy," he muttered. To Captain Pittman, he yelled, "Pittman, tell your man to stand down. We're calling in for instructions."

In a moment, the OUP Special Forces squad stood down and Sheriff Elswick and his men disappeared into the cellar.

Mostyn trotted over to where Jones had set up the LORSCOM just outside the front door to the ruined mansion.

"How're you coming?"

Jones looked up. "They're tracking down Bardon."

"Okay, let me know when you get him. I'm going to be in the cellar. I suppose that's where Kemper and Baker are, with Mansfield.

"Yep."

"Two deputies inside with Ohse?"

"Yep. ME is on his way, apparently."

"Thanks. I'll be in the cellar."

"Gotcha, Boss."

Mostyn made his way to the cellar entrance. Pittman, his men, their equipment, and the small surveillance robots were waiting.

Before Mostyn could say a word, the captain said, "Well?"

"Waiting for word from a higher authority," Mostyn replied.

"Kemper, Mansfield and Baker down there?"

"They followed the sheriff and his men."

"Let's go and see what's what. Special Agent Jones will let me know when we get in contact with Bardon."

Mostyn descended into the cellar. Pittman and his men followed. At the bottom of the steps, Mostyn told Pittman to follow him and he led the special forces team to the tunnel entrance. There he found Kemper, Mansfield, and Baker waiting.

"The sheriff and his men went on down," Kemper said.

Mostyn shook his head. "Crazy bastard. And I see he's swept the broken glass out of the way." He turned to Pittman. "Can your robots negotiate these steps?"

Pittman called out, "Neumeyer! Can the bots negotiate these steps?"

A Special Forces agent separated himself from the others and took a close look at the stairway. "Yes, sir, they should negotiate them just fine. We could carry the bots down. Save on the battery."

"What do you think, Mostyn?" Pittman asked.

"I think we should send one down to keep track of the sheriff and his men."

"Neumeyer, you and Thomas take one of the bots down. Set up a relay feed so we can watch from up here."

"Yes, sir," Neumeyer said.

In a few minutes the relay and screen were set up for Pittman and the others to observe. Neumeyer and Thomas then carried one of the bots down the long staircase and setup the control station for the bot. While they were doing that, the other two bots were brought into the room.

Over a walkie-talkie, Pittman gave the command and Neumeyer put the flat, caterpillar tracked machine in motion. The robot's floodlight illuminated the tunnel. The camera and microphone relayed the video and audio feed back to Neumeyer and on to Pittman. Mostyn watched, looking over the captain's shoulder. The tunnel was empty. However, the audio feed picked up the sound of distant voices.

"The locals must be quite a ways up the tunnel," Pittman commented.

"Good to know they're still alive," Mostyn said.

"You think these things are going to attack a dozen armed men?"

"Does a bear know if you have a rifle?"

"I see your point," the captain said.

"I hope they don't hurt them," Mansfield said.

"Who doesn't hurt whom?" Mostyn asked.

"I hope that crazy sheriff doesn't hurt the creatures."

"Doc, I have a feeling it's the sheriff and his men we

need to worry about." Mostyn turned back to the screen. "Can't that thing go any faster?"

"Full speed drains the battery faster," Pittman said.

"Of course."

Mostyn, Pittman, Mansfield, Baker, and Kemper crowded around the computer screen and watched the video as the robot rolled on down the tunnel. The pictures coming across the screen showed nothing but an empty tunnel. The audio, however, picked up the sound of voices. Indistinct, but definitely fragments of conversation.

"Have you been counting the side tunnels?" Mostyn asked Pittman.

"Yes. Five so far."

"Five? How far has that thing gone?"

"About a half-mile."

"Elswick and his men must be really hoofing it down there," Baker said.

"Without backup they're going to get themselves into trouble," Kemper said.

Mostyn nodded. "Agreed. The entire mountain might be honeycombed with tunnels. And it looks like the main tunnel has gotten wider. That will make it easier for the creatures to attack."

"*Attack of the Mole People*," Pittman said.

"If only this were a B grade sci-fi movie," Mostyn added.

Mansfield huffed. "They aren't 'mole people'. They're abhumans."

Pittman looked at him. "So what the hell is an abhuman and how did they get that way?"

"In the case of these people that is difficult to say, until we examine them," Mansfield replied. He went on, "Off-hand, my guess is extreme isolation and perhaps even loneliness caused a deterioration of mental capacity and moral fiber. Inbreeding sped the physical and mental regression to the bestial. You see, Captain, at base we are all animals. It isn't uncommon for extreme cases of mental illness to strip away the civilized and leave only the base mammal that is what all of us truly are."

"So are you saying being alone caused this?" Baker asked.

"In a manner of speaking, yes," Mansfield replied. "We have a family. A family is a micro-community. All communities wish to survive. Loneliness and isolation, especially if accompanied by persecution or paranoia, can cause the community to turn in upon itself. So this family, it would seem, did exactly that. Social mores broke down in the face of the instinct to survive. Incest became common practice. At least that is my guess. Which led to further degeneration." Mansfield shrugged. "But we won't know for sure until we examine them."

Gunshots sounded through the audio feed and strident, panic-filled voices.

Pittman stood. "All right, men, let's go. We got a fight on our hands. Time to save the locals."

Mostyn nodded his agreement and the OUP Special Forces unit raced down the steps and into the tunnel system. Neumeyer remained at the controls of the surveillance bot. Mostyn and the others watched as the bot picked up speed. The tunnel walls and floor zipped by.

Jones appeared in the room. "Boss, finally got hold of

Bardon. Explained the situation and he's pulling strings. I moved the LORSCOM. It's just outside the cellar entrance."

"All right, Jones. We have a situation down there."

Yelling and gunfire were coming through the audio feed. The bot sped around a curve in the tunnel and ran into a big furry body. There was a howl and from the video feed it was obvious the bot was in the air. There was a sound of metal against stone and then the video went blank.

From the walkie-talkie, Neumeyer's voice informed them the forward video camera was out and he was switching to the rear video camera. A picture appeared, revealing more furry shapes coming down the tunnel.

The audio was filled with human voices and animal sounds and gunfire. The bot was apparently being lifted into the air again and then the video showed a rapid descent and both video and audio went dead.

A frown appeared on Jones's face. "That can't be good."

Kemper rolled her eyes. "Duh."

Jones left and Neumeyer appeared in the doorway to the tunnel, slightly out of breath from the long climb. Faint sounds of gunfire could be heard in the quiet of the room.

"Should we send another bot down, sir?" Neumeyer asked.

"Yes," Mostyn replied.

Baker volunteered to help the Special Forces agent carry the robot down the stairs and Neumeyer sent the thing off at full tilt down the tunnel.

Mostyn, Kemper, and Mansfield watched the bot speed away from them towards the sound of the fighting, walls and floor zipping by. But what they weren't prepared for was the first indications things weren't going well for the men in the tunnel system. The bot's video feed picked up two Special Forces agents running hell for leather towards the stairs. The audio feed picking up the words "slaughter", "ambush", and "all dead".

In a few moments the bot came upon a scene of carnage. Scores of dead creatures, OUP agents, and deputies.

"Dotty," Mostyn's voice was filled with tension. "Tell Jones to put out an automated mayday. Then the two of you get into the front room of the house. Barricade the hallway entrance. We'll join you shortly."

She hesitated for a moment, then kissed Mostyn's cheek, and ran out of the room.

"Well, Doc, looks like 'first do no harm' ain't happening today."

"This is a disaster," Mansfield said, his face and tone of voice were glum.

"Especially for the homo sapiens amongst us. You join Kemper and Jones."

Mansfield hesitated.

"Now, Doctor."

He nodded and left.

Mostyn turned back to the console. The bot wasn't moving. In the video feed he saw furry shapes trotting in the direction of the stairway and the audio was sending back sounds more simian than human, and yet Mostyn sensed there were patterns to the simian sounds. Like those of speech.

Baker and Neumeyer burst into the room. "It's a rout," Neumeyer yelled.

On their heels were two Special Forces agents, their faces white with fear. One of them, voice trembling, said, "They're all dead."

"Baker, take them to the front room."

"Right," he replied, and led the men out of the cellar.

Mostyn looked around in the light provided by the lamps Pittman's men had set up. There wasn't much to block off the entrance. But there was the discarded junk and Mostyn decided that was better than nothing. First, though, he pushed the third bot down the stairway, and followed it up with the console and screen. Then he tossed down broken chairs, a small end table, a box of odds and ends. Whatever he could lift, he tossed into the opening to slow the advance of the creatures. He doubted anymore of Pittman's men or any of Elswick's party were coming out alive.

He looked over the pile of junk. There wasn't anything left he could handle on his own. So he swept as much of the glass as he could back into the doorway, and then tossed the big battery powered lamps down the steps. When that was done, it was time to leave. He took his pistol out of his holster, flipped on his flashlight, and made his way out of the cellar.

The night was dark. A crescent moon shown just above the treetops. The LORSCOM was beeping out the mayday signal.

A snap sounded in the night. Mostyn spun to his right. The flashlight picked up eyes, human and at the same time feral. The creature flinched in the light. Mostyn fired his pistol one-handed at the thing and took off running. Something was closing in on his right. He fired blindly and kept on running. He rounded the corner of the house. Jones was there with a shotgun and a brilliant lamp.

"Down!" Jones yelled.

Mostyn hit the ground and Jones fired. Pumped the shotgun and fired a second time.

"Okay, Boss, get in." Jones had his back to the wall, eyes and shotgun sweeping the area.

Mostyn ran into the house and Jones followed.

"Barricade the door!" Mostyn ordered.

The Special Forces agents were only too happy to comply.

"There was some neat equipment, the Special Forces guys didn't take with them," Jones said. "Kemper and I brought some of it in."

"What do we have?" Mostyn asked.

"Couple more shotguns, two MP-40s, three rifles with bayonets, stun grenades, tear gas grenades, glow sticks, and a half-dozen stun batons. Look like cattle prods, if you ask me."

"What would you know about a cattle prod, Jones?" Kemper said, her voice mocking in tone.

"Well, Miss Know-It-All, I happen to have worked on a cattle ranch for two summers," Jones shot back. "Here, let me use one on you to prove I'm not lying."

Jones picked one up and Dotty pointed her pistol at him.

"Enough!" Mostyn yelled. "Jesus, you two are worse than spoiled children."

Jones chuckled and put the stun baton down.

To the deputies, Mostyn asked, "You two are Tyler and Dempsey?"

Tyler nodded and Dempsey raised his hand.

Mostyn turned to the two Special Forces men he didn't know. "Your names?"

"Jack Zabaglioni," the medium height, slightly pudgy agent said.

"Phil Rankin," the other man said. He was tall and lanky in build.

Mostyn nodded to each. "Everyone arm up with the extra equipment. There are ten of us and God knows how many of them. Hopefully our mayday has been heard and the cavalry is on its way. We may have to hold out until sunrise, which is when these creatures will probably retreat underground."

Mostyn turned to Mansfield, "Am I right, Doc?"

"Yes, I believe so."

Mostyn continued. "So stay alert. Remember there are only the quick and the dead."

The lanterns were bright and caused sharp shadows to be cast against the wall. Mostyn thought they had a certain eeriness about them. Everyone took up defensive positions by the six windows. The silence was oppressive.

A loud thump sounded against the main door, but the barricade held. There was snarling and baying and then glass and wood flew into the room, along with a hairy and wild-eyed manlike beast.

13

─────

TYLER FIRED his .357 magnum revolver at the creature as it was getting up off the floor. It collapsed in a heap. Dempsey emptied his revolver at the shapes trying to clamber in through the open window and Tyler emptied his, as well. The bodies piled up and on they came.

On the other side of the room, another creature cannonballed through the glass and shutters. The small humanoid rolled and jumped up. Kemper put a bullet through its head. Another was coming through the window. Kemper fired a double-tap and the thing collapsed on the sill. She pushed it back the way it had come.

An abhuman took a swipe at her. She dodged and fired her pistol. The creature grunted and staggered back from the opening. A second bullet put it down. Right behind it was another and a double-tap from Kemper's pistol stopped it from entering.

With Tyler and Dempsey reloading, Jones fired two

blasts with his shotgun and followed up with a stun grenade. After that, all was quiet.

"I suppose it's wishful thinking to think we've scared them off," Baker said.

Mansfield looked deep in thought.

"What is it, Doc?" Mostyn asked.

"These beings." He'd stooped next to one of the bodies. "They seem to combine human rationality with the fearsomeness of a bestial predator. I would love to capture one."

"I don't think that's going to happen," Deputy Tyler said.

"I suppose not," Mansfield replied. "To study one, though, would be the chance of a lifetime."

"All right, people," Mostyn began, "no more surprises. Open the shutters. We're going to stop them before they reach us."

Shutters and windows were opened. At each of the front windows, two men were positioned. One on each side of the opening. The big electric lamp Jones had set outside the front door was still illuminating the overgrown yard and drive. At one of the side windows, was Kemper. At the other, was Jones. These were narrower windows, and only one of the abhumans could enter at a time. And with some difficulty at that. Jones stood to one side of his window. Kemper kneeled down behind the wall and peered over the sill.

A chorus of bloodcurdling screams rent the air and the creatures stormed the house. While some tried to force their way through the windows, others were trying to force the main door and the hall door.

Baker emptied his pistol and momentarily cleared the window for Mostyn to take a position right in front of the opening, where he emptied the magazine on the MP-40 submachine gun into the oncoming horde.

Neumeyer leaned out his window and used his MP-40 to thin out the creatures trying to force the front door, while Zabaglioni used three-round bursts from his M16 to keep the creatures away from the window. When the magazine was empty, Neumeyer tossed a tear gas grenade out the window to force the creatures back.

Again all was quiet, but not for long. Rocks started pelting the side of the house. One went through the window and hit Mansfield on the shoulder. Another caught Zabaglioni on the head and he collapsed onto the floor. There was a crash, the sound of breaking glass, and the flood light went out.

Rankin yelled, "Z's down. Breathing, but out. Took a rock to the head."

The rock barrage continued for a few more moments and then stopped. Mostyn ordered the lamps to be set outside the windows to better see the enemy approaching. That started another rock barrage and Dempsey replied with two shotgun blasts. However, the creatures succeeded in knocking out the lanterns.

Jones called out, "Boss, want to use the light sticks?"

Mostyn thought a moment and said to go ahead.

Everyone grabbed a couple glow sticks, bent them, shook them, and threw them out the windows.

"At least we'll catch them when they walk across the lights," Rankin said.

"Right," was Mostyn's reply, and then he asked about ammunition. The replies indicated everyone had little left.

After half an hour, the glow sticks began to dim.

"Keep alert," Mostyn advised. "If they're going to make a move, now will be the time."

"How many of these things, are there? They must breed like rabbits," Tyler said.

Kemper laughed. "According to Mansfield, they still have human instincts and humans love sex. Or haven't you noticed, Deputy?"

Mostyn asked about Zabaglioni.

Rankin said, "Breathing, but still out. The bleeding's stopped. Thank goodness."

Howling rent the air.

"Here they come," Rankin yelled and opened fire.

Pistols, rifles, submachine guns, and shotguns blazed a wall of lead and yet for every one of the things that fell, another took its place. Jones and Mostyn tossed stun and tear gas grenades out the windows. Those held off the onslaught for a time, but a new wave of the monstrosities charged the crumbling mansion.

One by one the guns fell silent. Jones and Rankin threw the last of the stun grenades and followed them up with the tear gas. The creatures fell back.

"All right, people," Mostyn began, "now it gets personal. Grab the stun batons, use your weapon as a club and those M-16s with the bayonets as spears. And if you have a knife, get ready to use it."

"Why am I getting the feeling this is turning out to be another Little Bighorn?" Baker said.

"It isn't," Mostyn replied.

Jones snapped and shook two glow sticks and tossed them to the back of the room.

"Jones, help me remove the blockade from the hall door."

"Okay, Boss."

"Get ready for any surprises," Mostyn said.

He and Jones removed the furniture barring the door. It flew open and four abhumans rushed into the room. Neumeyer and Rankin zapped them with the stun batons and down they went. Dempsey bayoneted, while Kemper cut their throats with surgical precision.

"Grab your stuff," Mostyn ordered. "Hoof it up the stairs. We'll have a better chance higher up. It'll be easier to defend the stairs."

Jones picked up Zabaglioni in a fireman's carry and everyone climbed the stairs to the second floor.

A wild howl rent the night air.

"Here they come," Mostyn said.

And then all was quiet. The sound of bare feet padded throughout the house. First one pair of feet and then another sounded on the stairs. Mostyn and Jones were waiting at the top off to the side.

The first creature reached the top and stood on the second floor landing. The second, was on the second step from the top. Jones and Mostyn lunged. Jones got his knife into the thing's neck and made a sideways move to the front of the throat. The blade severed the vocal chords, arteries, and veins. The creature collapsed to the floor without a sound and quickly bled out.

Mostyn wasn't so lucky. He misjudged the distance in the dark and the thing let out a cry of surprise before Mostyn could silence it.

There was an explosion of howling and yelping guttural growls. The beasts started up the stairs. Mostyn pushed his victim and the body tumbled down onto the monsters streaming up the staircase.

Jones grabbed the other body and threw it into the oncoming mob, scattering the creatures attempting to reach the second floor like bowling pins.

However, that didn't stop the abhumans for long. Back up the stairs they came. Mostyn, Jones, and Dempsey held them off with the stun sticks until the number of creatures on the stairs was so numerous they were like a battering ram and simply pushed their way onto the landing.

Mostyn slashed one of the thing's gut open. Kemper slit a throat. Jones, using the shotgun as a club, bashed in a head. Rankin, Baker, and Tyler bayoneted beast after beast. And as more of the things broke out onto the floor, Mansfield and Neumeyer went to work with stun batons and knives.

The creatures were like a flood and Mostyn ordered a retreat up to the third floor. They could not take the unconscious Zabaglioni with them, and Tyler got separated from the group. His cries for help were filled with terror and then they abruptly ceased.

To make matters worse, one by one the batteries in the stun batons went dead. Neumeyer, wielding his as a club, smashed in the side of one thing's head. Rankin jammed his bayonet into one beast's eye. But the human-like beasts kept on coming. Abhuman pushing human up the stairs to the third floor.

Rankin was grabbed by a hand and pulled into the sea of hairy human-like things. He screamed once and was silent. Neumeyer and Dempsey jabbed away at face and throat, the staircase too narrow to allow for an effective swing. Behind them were Mostyn and Jones.

Step by step, the abhumans pushed up the staircase. Neumeyer jabbed one in the throat, while a hairy hand from another grabbed his shirt. A quick jab in the eye from Mostyn saved the Special Forces agent from disappearing into the yowling, stinking, hairy sea of humanoids.

Mostyn yelled, "Kemper, Baker, Mansfield find us a room and get ready to barricade the door."

The abhumans had now pushed the humans up to the third floor. Mostyn, Jones, Dempsey, and Neumeyer spread out. Shotgun, stun baton, and knives went to work with savage efficiency. Abhumans fell, but the humans weren't unscathed. Neumeyer was bleeding from a bad bite. Dempsey had numerous wounds made by the creatures's claws. Jones, too, had been clawed. Mostyn was bleeding from numerous cuts.

Kemper yelled, "Now! We're ready!"

The men broke and ran for the room. Mostyn, though, letting Dempsey get to safety, got caught at the door. One of the abhumans held his leg and another had hold of his arm. Mostyn screamed as the thing bit his arm.

Kemper hurled an old ewer and hit the creature that

had Mostyn's arm. It's grip loosened and Mostyn wrenched his arm free, then elbowed the thing in the face. He flipped his knife around and stabbed backwards. The blade slashed the thing's neck and arterial spray went everywhere.

Baker bayoneted a beast reaching for Mostyn. Mansfield slashed the fingers of the creature holding Mostyn's leg and Jones pulled him into the room. Neumeyer slammed the door shut and threw the bolt. Dempsey and Kemper shoved the bed against the door and then Jones and Dempsey piled a chest of drawers on top of the bed.

From outside the room, they heard the whump-whump of a chopper and soon a searchlight was shining on the house, moving window by window along the building.

Kemper shouted, "I need something white!"

Neumeyer stripped off his shirt and gave her his undershirt.

She had a window open and frantically waved the white shirt to catch the attention of the people in the helicopter. Suddenly she was bathed in the bright light of the searchlight.

An amplified voice informed them help was coming. In a moment, the air shimmered and a dark-haired, pale-skinned woman materialized before them. In her arms was a sonic disruptor.

She turned to Mostyn. "Hello, my husband. I've come to rescue you."

14

"WHAT THE FUCK IS THIS?" Kemper blurted out.

Mostyn sighed.

Jones laughed. "Don't look a gift K'n-yanian in the mouth, Kemper."

Her look was venomous. "Wish to God we'd left her in that subterranean hellhole."

Footsteps sounded on the roof.

"Good to see you, H'tha-dub," Mostyn said.

The K'n-yanian came up to him and lightly kissed his lips. "Helene, my sweet. I'm Helene in your world."

"Right."

She sent her thoughts to him. "I've missed you, my love, but now I'm here."

Mostyn sent his thoughts back. "And I've missed you, too."

Out loud, Helene said, "With this weapon, I will protect you while you escape."

"What the hell is it?" Dempsey asked.

"A sonic disruptor," Jones said.

"What's it do?" the deputy asked.

"Basically uses sound to disrupt the molecular structure," Jones replied.

"There are such things?" Incredulity was written all over the deputy's face.

Jones clapped him on the shoulder. "Welcome to the dark side of your government." Then with a big grin on his face, he said, "We're the Feds, and we're going to help you."

Dempsey looked skeptical. "I doubt that. But if this thing will save our asses, who am I to complain?"

Helene smiled. "I and this weapon will save your asses."

And, as if in response, there was a loud bang on the door, and bed and dresser jumped.

"Are they using a battering ram?" Baker asked.

"Sounds like it," Jones said.

Mansfield rubbed his hands together. "My God, these creatures are astounding."

"Tell me how astounding they are after they've bitten *your* face off," Dempsey said.

There was another bang, followed by two more in succession. Another loud bang and the door splintered. The next sound was that of a sledgehammer breaking through the heavy door. From the roof came the sound of a saw.

Two more blows successfully turned the upper half of the door into kindling.

"My God!" Mansfield exclaimed. "They retain the knowledge of the use of tools."

Helene flipped a switch and the sonic disruptor began to hum and the rings along the barrel lit up. It looked for all the world like something out of a 1930s Buck Rogers movie.

Through the opening the group could see the creatures slam a large wooden log against the door. The dresser and bed jumped back another few inches. The saw continued cutting through the boards of the roof. Another loud bang and there was the sound of splintering wood. The dresser and bed were shoved further into the room.

Through the opening came a cascade of rocks. Baker and Mansfield each getting hit.

Helene raised the disruptor. A square of roof boards dropped to the floor followed by a collapsible ladder.

"Everybody up," Mostyn ordered. "Kemper first."

Kemper started up. "Staying with the wifey?" she asked, her voice dripping acid.

Mostyn ignored her. "Baker and Mansfield next. Then you, Dempsey, Neumeyer."

The bed and dressers slid across the floor, and Helene pulled the trigger. A high-pitched whine sounded and the disruptor beam, set to wide angle, cut through the barricades, the wall, splintered remnants of the door, and a number of the abhumans. Only a fine dust remained.

The creatures were stunned, and stood staring at where their companions, the door, and wall had been.

Jones laughed. "That surprised them. Just you, me, and Helene, Boss."

"Up you go, Jones."

Mostyn reached for the weapon. "Now you, Helene."

"Oh, no, my love. You go."

The creatures threw rocks and charged. Helene pull the trigger, reducing them to a fine dispersal of molecules.

"I can dematerialize. Go, my husband, before they attack again."

Reluctantly, Mostyn ascended the ladder and just before he was on the roof he looked back. The creatures surged forward. The disruptor didn't fire. Mostyn watched Helene disappear in a sea of hairy bodies.

Mostyn screamed her name, but she was gone. He climbed out onto the roof and standing before him was Helene Dubreuil.

EPILOGUE

THE SURVIVORS SPENT two days debriefing. All except for Arliss Cashel, because she wasn't in the final battle. When the debriefing was over, Deputy Dempsey, because of what he'd seen of OUP operations, was given an offer he couldn't refuse and joined the OUP. Even though the offer was tantamount to coercion, he didn't mind overly much, because his new pay grade was significantly higher than what he made as a deputy.

The body count of the abhumans had been extremely high. Nevertheless, many remained and Doctor Mansfield got his wish. OUP Special Forces captured over two dozen of the creatures and transported them to a secret Federal facility where Mansfield would be able to study them with a high-level scientific team.

DNA testing of the captured abhumans confirmed that the things were the direct descendants of the Vander Vrooman family that had moved to Tyler County in the early 1800s.

Doctor Bardon sat behind his desk, across from Doctors Kemper and Mansfield, Mostyn, and Helene Dubreuil. He was giddy with excitement and puffed away on his pipe.

"Well, well, well. What an adventure." He set his pipe down. "Doctor Mansfield, I'm sure you feel much satisfaction knowing your theory of human degeneration appears to be valid."

"I do indeed. And that evolution itself may reverse direction. We aren't guaranteed unlimited advancement. There may be regression too."

"And now you have the opportunity to also work with the team observing the Martenses."

Mansfield was all smiles. "Thank you for that, Doctor Bardon."

The director simply shook his head. "Governments can be so idiotic at times. There was no reason, other than departmental politics, to have excluded us from the Martense research."

"Indeed not," Mansfield concurred.

"And now are you a believer, Doctor Kemper?" Bardon inquired.

"The evidence is difficult to argue against," she replied.

"Good. Good. You'll get to study the dead creatures which we've transported to your special laboratory."

"Thank you, sir."

"I expect you and Doctor Mansfield will share information," Bardon said.

"Of course, sir," Kemper replied.

"I look forward to working with you, Doctor Kemper," Mansfield said.

Bardon turned to Mostyn. "I'm sorry for the losses. Sheriff Elswick was rash and Captain Pittman not much better, and he's the one who should have known better. But then who could have guessed how cunning the Vander Vrooman abhumans were?" He turned to Mansfield. "Right, Doctor?"

"Very much so."

With a twinkle in his eye, Bardon looked at Mostyn. "Per your request, I've gotten Mr. Gillies a job with a private security firm."

"Thank you, sir," Mostyn replied.

Dotty Kemper's face was a picture of puzzlement. "How did you work that out, sir?"

Bardon had a smile on his face. "The firm does work for us on occasion."

Kemper nodded. "Of course."

The director turned his attention to Mansfield. "Well, I won't keep you any longer, Doctor Mansfield. I'm sure you're champing at the bit to get at your new work."

"Yes, sir." Mansfield stood, shook hands with Bardon and Mostyn, and bid everyone farewell.

With Mansfield gone, Bardon's gaze took in Mostyn, Kemper, and Dubreuil. "An exciting adventure. You distinguished yourselves, as usual. And especially you, Helene, in your first field operation."

The three thanked their boss for his praise.

Bardon looked over at the statues of Cthulhu and Shub-Niggurath that had been taken from a previous operation in the subterranean world of K'n-yan. "Unless, of course, we count you coming here, Helene, as your first operation."

She smiled. "I do not think so, sir. I was merely following my heart back then."

"Yes, indeed." A smile touched his lips. "Have you ladies told him?"

"Not yet," Kemper answered.

Bardon stood. "I need to chat a moment with Evelyn. If you'll excuse me." He left the room.

"Shall you or I?" Helene asked.

"I will," Dotty replied.

"Tell me what?" Mostyn's voice was laced with suspicion.

Dotty cleared her throat. "We've decided to share you."

"What?"

"You heard me, Mostyn. Don't pretend you're deaf. Helene and I are going to share you. We decided alternating months would work best."

"Wait a minute. Don't *I* get a say in the matter?"

"Look Mostyn, you love both of us and don't pretend you don't. Helene loves you. Shit, she came to a totally different world just to be with you. And I, well, I… Ah, shit, I'll just say it. I love you. And have for a long time. Bardon's concerned our little triangle is going to mess up his 'best people', as he put it."

"This was Bardon's idea?"

"Not exactly," Helene said. "But he wanted Dotty and I to come to a decision. So we did. Neither of us wished to give you up to the other."

"Not that I'm into sharing," Dotty said. "However, joint custody with alternating visitation I think might work. And

Bardon said he has an ancient Egyptian book of spells that might help us if we need it."

"Good grief. So this was Bardon."

"No," Dotty said. "We came up with this on our own."

Mostyn thought to himself, *sure they did*.

"So now, Mostyn Pierce," Helene began, calling him the name she used in the subterranean world of K'n-yan, "I won the toss of the coin. I get you first."

Mostyn looked at Dotty. "Seriously, you're okay with this?"

"I'm okay, Pierce. I have all those bodies I need to examine. They'll keep me busy and when it's my turn, I'll be looking for a break."

There was a knock on the door and Bardon entered. He walked to his desk and sat. "Everything okay? Mostyn?"

He looked at Dotty, and looked at Bardon for a few moments before answering. "Uh, sure, I guess so."

"Good. Very good. Well, why don't you three be getting along. You have work to do, Doctor Kemper," and, directing his gaze to Mostyn and Helene, "you two have some reacquainting to do. Been a while since you were together."

Kemper, Mostyn, and Dubreuil stood, said goodbye, and left.

Bardon picked up his pipe and re-lit it. He leaned back in his chair and puffed on the old bent bulldog briar. His gaze took in the hideous statues on either end of his sideboard.

A smile played on his lips. "I just love Egyptian magic."

A WORD FROM CW

I hope you enjoyed *Terror in the Shadows*.

If you did, please leave a review where you bought the book and on your favorite social media sites. Your review is like word of mouth advertising. And it is pure gold.

Enter my World

Enter my world. A world of terror on a cosmic scale. Just click, tap, or scan the QR code below.

Fear is the most primal of human emotions. And fear of the unknown is the most terrifying of all fears.

If you are new to the Pierce Mostyn Paranormal Investigations series, then *Terror in the Shadows* is an excellent entry point into the series and into my world.

In addition to my Pierce Mostyn Paranormal Investigations books, I've written short stories set in the world of the macabre and arcane. Many of which are only available to folks on my mailing list.

So just click, tap, or scan the QR code to enter my world of terror and the macabre. You will get a free copy of *The Feeder* and you'll get my monthly email of news and curated contact. Terror awaits!

CONTINUE THE ADVENTURE!

The paranormal investigations of Pierce Mostyn continue in *Van Dyne's Vampires*.

Evil genius and mad scientist Valdis Damien Van Dyne has created a new super monster: a vampiric entity moldable to local legends.

Can Pierce Mostyn stop Van Dyne before the new monster goes into large scale production and the governments of the world are destabilized?

Van Dyne's Vampires is available at your favorite online store. Check it out! Just click, tap, or scan the QR code.

BOOKS BY CW HAWES

CW is a multi-genre author.

The books below are portals to his many exciting worlds. And no AI was used in the writing of these books. Books by a human for a human.

Justinia Wright Private Investigator Mysteries

Justinia Wright is the PI with panache. These slow burn mysteries, written in homage to Rex Stout's Nero Wolfe, are sure to satisfy your craving for intriguing puzzles, quirky characters, and wise-cracking humor.

Vampire House and Other Early Cases of Justinia Wright, PI
Festival of Death
Trio in Death-Sharp Minor
But Jesus Never Wept
The Conspiracy Game
A Nest of Spies

When Friends Must Die
Death Makes a House Call
To Right a Wrong
The Nine Deadly Dolls
Ripples on the Pond
Christmas with the Wrights
Minneapolis's Finest
Jack in the Box
Sauerkraut Days
Justinia Wright Private Investigator Omnibus Edition

Magnolia Bluff Crime Chronicles

Tense slow burn mysteries set in our favorite town in the Texas Hill Country.

Death Wears a Crimson Hat
Ten Million Ways to Die
Who Mourns Elektra?
Death by Moonlight

Pierce Mostyn Paranormal Investigations

The X-Files meets Cthulhu. Pierce Mostyn does battle with inter-dimensional monsters bent on the destruction of humanity.

Nightmare in Agate Bay
Stairway to Hell
Terror in the Shadows
Van Dyne's Vampires
The Medusa Ritual

Demons in the Dunes
Van Dyne's Zuvembies
In the Shadow of the Mountains of Madness

The Rocheport Saga

A post-apocalyptic adventure series in the style of cozy catastrophes such as *Earth Abides* and *Day of the Triffids*. Join Bill Arthur as he strives to build a new and better world on the ashes of the old.

The Morning Star
The Shining City
The Divided City
The Troubled City
By Leaps and Bounds
Freedom's Freehold
Take to the Sky

Decopunk

Alternative history adventures in a world where World War II never happened and swing is still king.

From the Files of Lady Dru Drummond
The Moscow Affair
The Golden Fleece Affair

Rand Hart Adventures
Rand Hart and the Pajama Putsch

Tales of the Macabre

For the horror lover in you.
Do One Thing For Me
Metamorphosis
What the Next Day Brings
Ancient History

Anthologies

Enjoy CW's stories in these short story collections.
The Phantom Games
Beyond the Sea
Overmorrow
Arachnapocalypse! The Anthology
Once Upon a WolfPack

Available at your favorite online retailer. Just click, tap, or scan the QR code to be taken to My Books page for buy links.

ABOUT CW HAWES

CW Hawes has written over 50 novels and shorter works of fiction. He was also a successful poet and had over 200 poems appear in ezines and and print.

He is a founding member of the Underground Authors and was the impetus for the highly successful Magnolia Bluff Crime Chronicles series.

After 35 years of working in county government, he retired at the beginning of 2015 and began a second career as a fictioneer. Perhaps some of some of the horrors Pierce Mostyn faces can be traced to his creator's own experiences in county government and beyond. Perhaps.

CW lives in Southern California. He enjoys reading, writing, chess and other board games, his daily morning walk, and contemplating the meaning of life while smoking his pipe. He also hasn't met a doughnut or a pizza he doesn't like, is something of a tea snob, and rocks out to Handel and Vaughan Williams.

You can get curated content and the occasional free story

when you join his mailing list, and you can reach him at his website, on X, and also Facebook.

To join his mailing list, click, tap, or scan the QR code:

To visit him on his website, click, tap, or scan the QR code:

To visit him on X, click, tap, or scan the QR code:

To visit him on Facebook, click, tap, or scan the QR code: